FILLING

UP

IN

CUMBY

AND

OTHER

STORIES

ALSO BY JIM STEINBERG

BOUNDARIES

LAST NIGHT AT THE VISTA CAFÉ
STORIES

FILLING UP IN CUMBY

AND OTHER STORIES

Jim Steinberg

Arcata, California

For John "Moose" Mason for his perfect friendship

CONTENTS

AN APPLE TOTEM

IT WAS TIME TO GO. The man had finished loading the contents of his boy's room into the old Toyota wagon. In boxes packed tight against each other were his clothes, games, toys and books; his collections of rocks, cards, feathers and school-made art; his first computer, first record player, and the hand-me-down tape deck. Visible through the windows, stuffed into spaces between the boxes, were the dying remote control car, the flattened box kite that doubled as a mobile, and the homemade bows and arrows and other artifacts from the life of a ten-year-old. On the luggage rack were the boy's first pair of skis and his custom-made pine bed-desk, its dismantled pieces cinched together and held down with ropes and bungee cords. The boy's red and black dirt bike, his most prized possession, hung on a rack at the back of the wagon. Everything he owned was there.

From the deck in front of his bedroom, the man stared down at the load and contemplated the inevitable next step. Not twenty feet away behind the parted French doors, the boy sat at his father's oak desk, his back to the doors, busy at something and quite serious about it.

The pieces of the custom-made bed-desk caught the man's attention and held it. He imagined reassembling it in the boy's new room at his mother's house two hundred miles away. The structure would dwarf the little space, putting the boy close to that seven-foot ceiling at night in exchange for a small gain of space underneath, where the desk connected to one end of the elevated bed. His boy would need that extra space. It would expand the room enough for a good fort of blankets, a future friend's sleeping bag, an expansive Lego project. Just like we do here, the man hoped. Just like here.

The boy loved his single significant piece of furniture, a birthday surprise four years ago that the father had wanted to build himself. But he turned the project over to Jack English, his carpenter friend, when time ran out. In the late August afternoon of the birthday, while the boy worked on the earthen fort in the back pasture with his stepbrother, stepsister, and a pack of friends from town, Jack brought the bed-desk over in pieces through the front door. They assembled it in a rush so Jack could leave and the gift could materialize in the boy's room just about the time the kids would come in for hot dogs, cake, ice cream, and presents. The rush was unnecessary. In their tee shirts the kids worked into the cool, damp fog of a Northcoast summer evening, digging tunnels and trenches into the fresh mound of earth removed for the man's shop, blocking and fortifying the passages with old boards and two-by-fours, adding ramps to the summit. They camouflaged the raw embankments and wooden battlements with scrubby Scotch broom yanked from the pasture and fading green branches stripped from scraggly pines the father had taken down in search of sun and horizon. When his wife called in the builders, a table full of presents and the smell of hot dogs and French fries distracted the boy from the surprise in his room. A friend saw the bed-desk first and called him in.

"Awesome," the boy had said to his hovering father. He edged toward the door and his gang of friends waiting in the dining room for the mounds of food and stacks of presents, but not before their eyes met. The father nodded his blessing for the quick departure. He knew that after all the excitement he would find his boy arranging the desk and the shelves, fighting fatigue to get his treasures and supplies the way he wanted them before bedtime.

That night, after the boy had climbed the ladder for the first time and tucked himself in, he looked down at his father with hard-to-keep-open eyes under those long, curving lashes.

"Thanks, Dad. This bed is really cool." Then he patted his father on the top of the head, a few quick little pats with a stiffened palm like he had done so many times before. He closed his eyes and drifted away.

Standing there, the man pulled himself from his daydream. Wondering what his boy was doing at the desk, not a spot he often used, the man remembered that even back when Jack English made the bed-desk he knew this day was coming. But he hadn't begun counting down. Four years seemed like a long time. Oh, he thought now, how the years had shrunk to seasons, to months, to weeks, then to days and hours, now minutes. He turned and looked through the French doors. His boy was hunched over an apple, focusing on it with great concentration. The man decided to leave him alone.

He idled toward the end of the railing, where four broad steps led down to a lower deck that fronted the kitchen and dining room. Staring at the car below, he saw the ruddy old teddy bear from his own long ago, reincarnated now in his son's childhood, sitting erect between the bucket seats, perfectly centered. His boy had placed it there. He had never used the teddy for security in the cuddling sense, the man thought. In the uncertain early days of their blended family, he had stationed it atop a corner shelf overlooking the first collection of Lego outer space vehicles he had assembled with his stepbrother and stepsister. The fleet changed at least three times a year, but the teddy bear remained in place for nearly five. Today it sat again at center stage close to where the boy would sit on the journey to his next home. Nearly hairless after more than thirty years, the teddy seemed called upon to preside over still another change in the boy's life. That old falling apart critter, he thought, binds past to present, son to father.

He thought of the day a year and a half ago when his boy met Jack. They were taking their loaded '52 Chevy pickup to the city dump where Jack worked. Starting from the booth at the entry, Jack checked the size of their load to determine the charge. The boy watched Jack struggle to walk around the truck and measure the load with his eyes, pulling at his legs as if they had no joints and were filled with earth. The boy listened to their chatter, then met the man who built his bed-desk. Jack grinned and tried to hide the pain on his too-old face. He heaved himself onto the old truck's running board, clasped the boy's shoulder with knobby fingers on a stiff hand, and said he had a boy too, about the same age.

"That's the man who made my bed-desk?" his boy asked a few minutes later at the unloading dock. His eyes held wonder.

"That's Jack," the father answered. Why do you ask?"

"I don't know." He paused, looked back toward the booth where Jack was estimating another load. "He's really cool. How come you know him?"

"Met him right here, got to talking."

Their eyes met for an instant, and the boy nodded. The father decided it was enough, and left it there.

He walked down the deck stairs to check on the bed-desk bound to the top of the car. Tugging at the ropes and bungee cords, he decided it was secure, but the picture of it cramping his boy's new room hovered before him. He mounted the steps to regain his perch. The bed-desk, he thought, was another continuity he had woven through the changes his child had endured, more and harder changes than should distract a boy till he's older. What a wonder, he thought, that a father makes these choices without knowing what they are really for.

He thought about going back inside to visit his boy and see what his project was about, but he fought against it. On earlier trips from the Toyota to his boy's room, the father had detoured through the kitchen to stand at his bedroom door and stare. Each time the boy seemed nearly motionless at the big desk at the far end of the large room. This time he gave in. Wanting to be careful, he walked down the deck to the front door to approach him from the short set of stairs between his bedroom and the kitchen. He thought that would be sufficient distance.

With one hand the boy held a large green apple in a shaft of sunlight. With the other he moved a magnifying glass in slow circles over the apple's surface. The man noticed a wisp of smoke rising in front of his boy's face. He watched for a moment and wondered, thought better of being there, and started to leave. He would check the boy's closet one last time. But before he left he noticed the haze of dusty sunlight surrounding his boy. It seemed to suspend him in the distance of a far-off time and place. He knew there was no way to extend the seven years, nothing left to do but linger and watch for a little longer. But he didn't. It was time to go.

He took comfort that his boy did not seem nervous, but full of intention.

Outside, he tried thinking of items they might have left in other rooms. Standing under the shade of the cypress tree closest to the deck, he gave in once more to the relentless pulse of memory and let his eyes wander through the yard until they settled on the tire swing. A few years ago he had hung it from a swooping branch of the great tree as compensation to the kids for removing the lower branches that darkened the living room. Those muscular branches had been the kids' routes into the tree's grand interior, where without help they had built a tree house from discarded lumber. In a fit of chainsaw fever he had skinned the stumps too flat for climbing. A makeshift rope ladder never worked as well. The kids complained and abandoned their beloved tree house for the earthen battlements in the pasture. He had apologized for doing too clean a job on the branches, but they teased him long after.

He studied the pasture to the right of the front yard. The old red Chevy truck sat at its edge. They hadn't finished their summer chores: hauling blackberry vines and Scotch broom and pine branches to the burn pile or the bucked logs to the chopping block. For at least a few years now his boy helped him during the hauling in return for driving lessons, a fatherly bribe netting time together and an exercise in fair exchange. At first he only steered from his dad's lap but soon advanced to shifting gears while the man worked the pedals. When the boy couldn't quite handle loading and unloading tangled masses much larger than himself, he tried to match his steering time in other ways. He tossed small logs from atop the load and heaved a few bigger ones, swept out the truck bed, and did other chores that the father could not remember. The exchange of value ceased to matter. Driving became his boy's main job, on his father's lap, hands stretching for the wheel.

These are memories that might follow his boy, the man thought. He hoped they would outlast the items stuffed in the car and keep him connected with this time and place

and the family they had made here. He wondered when the
boy would begin to think about them in that way. Not right
now, he hoped. They'd only get in the way.

A twinge of guilt for breaking his son's life into
different pieces washed through him but left when he heard
a warm, whispered voice close behind him, then felt his
wife's hand on his shoulder.

"Maybe you should get started now," she said.

He turned into a waiting hug. "He's into one of his
projects," he muffled into her hair. "I want to let him finish."

"I've packed some sandwiches, but I suppose you
boys will stop at the Cave Junction Inn."

She squeezed tighter.

"The lousy coffee-junk food ritual," he said.

"He'll like it," she answered. "You're okay?"

"So long as I watch from a distance."

"He'll be okay, you know."

"I do."

"It's time now. Why don't you see if he wants to take
his project with him?"

He pulled out of the hug and thanked her. She was
so often right about what to do, so consistently a step ahead
of him, so gentle in her timing. He went inside feeling lucky
she would be here when he returned the next day, without
his boy.

At the bedroom door, the man stopped to watch his
son once more. The boy still sat in the shaft of light. So
trained on the apple were the boy's eyes, so deep was his
scrutiny, he did not notice his father watching. The
magnifying glass was down now, and the fingertips of the
boy's left hand fiddled with its handle as if they might in the
next moment pick it up or leave it there. How engrossed he
seemed. The father had expected a tougher passage through
this day, but his son had put himself under a spell of
concentration that seemed to free him, for the moment, from
the encumbrance of hard change. The difficult time would
come at the other end, he thought, or maybe now, when he
breaks the spell. He closed his eyes and took a breath. In the
darkness an insight startled him, a moment of recognition.
This was no escape he watched but a project driven from
within. His son was working against time toward something

important to this moment. He was sure of it.

The man opened his eyes and saw his son looking at him.

"Dad," he called. "Come up here."

The man climbed the four stairs and crossed the room. He watched his boy pick up the apple and close his fingers around it, hiding whatever he had burned into its side. His boy swiveled the oak chair sideways and extended his arm, puncturing the beam of light coming down next to him.

"This is for you, Dad," the boy said. He opened his fingers. The apple sat upon his flattened palm at the end of his outstretched arm. Something strong the father couldn't name, some intangible certainty, filled his son's wide-open eyes. The father paused to bathe in it, this gift passing with the apple in a ritual parting enacted for him. No, for us, he thought. That's what my boy's eyes are saying.

"Take it," the boy said.

The father obeyed and twisted the apple around. His name was burned into its side in neat brown capital letters half an inch high. A narrow band of the apple's inner flesh framed each letter. Around each of those was a band of unburned green skin.

"Thanks, Son," he said. "I don't know what to say. I think I know what this..."

"It's time to go, Dad." The boy rose from the chair, looked up, returned his father's gaze.

"This is a marker, isn't it?"

"It's gonna last a super long time."

"I love it. It's terrific."

The father held the apple aloft and stared at his name carved into its side by the light of the sun. It wouldn't last, he thought. He looked at his boy, into his eyes again, expecting to find a weakening there, a need for confirmation. He found only conviction.

"It's gonna dry up and shrink around your name. It'll get harder and harder and lighter and lighter but the letters won't change much. I think it's gonna look like a big raisin."

The father looked at the apple again, then back at his boy.

"It will, Dad."

"How do you know for sure?"

"I just do. You wait. Put it back on the desk, in the sun."

He looked out the window toward the sun the boy had used to write his name. It rode the edge of the fog, waiting to be covered. He placed the apple in the middle of the weakening circle of light on the desk's surface and thought about the trip up the coast. If the fog didn't come in too fast they might skirt it all the way past Crescent City, moving in and out of vague transitions of sun and shadow. The fog seemed to hasten the lives of most things, but it nursed the redwoods and kept them alive for a thousand years. Beyond Crescent City they'd turn inland into the narrow, rugged valley of the Smith River on the road he had driven dozens of times to take the boy or pick him up, but not like this. They would outrun the fog as it moved inland over the valley's clear, tumbling river, into Oregon and real summer. Just past the border they would snack at the Cave Junction Inn where so many visits had ended or begun. They would push on in time to eat a late dinner with the boy's mother. He would set up the bed-desk at a crazy hour, sleep on the futon couch in her living room, and have breakfast with them in the morning.

For a brief moment his ex-wife and he would parent together and hope for an easy departure and a smooth transition. They would notice their boy looking out the window in the bright mountain sunlight toward a boy playing by himself in a front yard across the street, a boy about the same age. Their boy would get on his red and black dirt bike and ride widening circles in the street, waiting for the path of his life to intersect that of a boy he did not know. Soon the two would start to play, and theirs would not look back toward the window that framed them. They would know that it was time. With a little push from the mother and a sandwich for the road, the man would put his bag in the car and walk up to his boy in the neighbor's yard for the last hug and the last goodbye. He wouldn't let it take much time. He would get in his car and creep down the hill, looking in the rearview mirror at the shrinking picture. The boy would see his father's wave and return it, hardly taking his attention from the possible new friend. The father would creep a few more front yards down the road before looking back one last time. The road and the yard would be empty.

He would try to drive home without stopping. He would race the Smith, dancing through its rocky gorges and tunnels of trees down to the sea. In the early afternoon the bank of fog would be coming in from the sea. Where the mountains come to the shore, the road would lift him above the gleaming fog and drop him back into the soft wisps of its moving, translucent border over and over again. The redwoods would dapple the sun's rays into shimmering bright spots on the ancient forest floor. At home his wife would hug him, keep an eye on him, wait for him to talk. He would sit at his desk and look at the apple and his name carved on its side. He would come back to it time and again, to hold it, turn it, and wonder how long it would last.

FILLING UP IN CUMBY

WE ARE CROSSING HIGH DESERT in eastern Oregon on a January night. A split-apart family of three, we are together at that moment by accident or design, depending on our different points of view. I'm hunched over the wheel watching for the next suicidal jackrabbit. Maggie sits in the shotgun seat with our five-year-old Trajan on her lap. When a jackrabbit starts across the road, she stiffens through my dodging and braking and yells, "Do something Jack!" then cringes or relaxes, depending on the results. Trajan's gestures mimic hers, but even as I concentrate on the next frozen animal, I can see adventure in his wide-open eyes.

It is after midnight. This high desert is new country I might have seen if not for the late start I allowed, for my own sake. The explosion of stars is some compensation, but the immediate situation presses hard: the gas tank needle approaches Big Ugly E; we haven't seen an open station in hours; we have at least fifty miles to the next town, a small dot on the map named Cumby, written in the smallest letters. My stomach churns with guilt for having raced through John Day without stopping for gas, and with discomfort at the prospect of not reaching Cumby. The heater works overtime to push out the January cold, and the January cold pushes back and whistles through the windows' worn seals. Trajan squirms on Maggie's lap. I look at him in his stiff little parka with its fur hood pulled close around his head almost to his eyes. Maggie wears her gloves.

"Jack, our feet are cold," she says in her low, throaty voice. Still lovely, that voice, even through my anger at her being here. "Switch to heat," she demands.

I bristle at her denial of the frosty evidence on the windshield. It brings forth the supreme irritations of the last two days and challenges the self-control I've imposed on myself for Trajan's sake. But she is too cold and entwined with him to easily reach the switch. I try to give her the benefit of the doubt, but I fail.

"I could switch to heat if we'd all stop breathing," I say, my discipline breaking down for one of the few times since Maggie joined us in Moscow and spoiled my first visit to Elizabeth, my maybe new girlfriend.

She gives me an unconcealed frown. Her eyes seem to search the side of my face, probing, I think, for a sign of anger. There is plenty of that, and I don't want her to see it. Or Trajan to see it.

"*My* feet aren't cold, Momma." Trajan is eating up being with his mother again. Too much time without her. And this night ride with its dark possibility remains unspoiled for him, at least for now. During the early stages of an adventure a boy's toes don't get cold, but Maggie and I are dangerously close to spoiling his future great tale of the race to Cumby against Big Ugly E. I want to preserve that for him, and I want him to have a good time with his mother.

Until this allegedly accidental encounter, Maggie and I have managed to keep Trajan mostly safe from our struggles, first to stay married, then to stay separated. We have not fought in his presence, outwardly or by innuendo. On this weary night, after this long day and the one before, I worry we may fail for the first time.

Trajan looks from Maggie to me. "Are we gonna run out of gas?"

"Probably," Maggie says.

He tries a frown, and Maggie self-corrects halfheartedly. "We're not too far from this Cumby place. We'll be okay."

"Yeah, we will," Trajan perks. "Dad will get us to the Cumby place."

"I came this way," Maggie says. "I don't remember it."

"Dad, do you remember the Cumby place?"

"We didn't come this way, but it's on the map." Inside I wonder will it be there, and if it is, will it have a pump? Places without pumps do show up on maps, and places on maps don't always show up on roads.

Trajan straightens up and stares through the window. "It's there, Mom."

Maggie nods and stares straight ahead. Trajan looks back and forth.

"That's right," I say. "Cumby is just ahead."

TRAJAN AND I LEFT Arcata, California a week ago to visit Elizabeth Montgomery in Moscow, Idaho. Elizabeth is my first . . . I don't know what to call her, I don't know if we will become something that deserves a different name than friends. I know this: I'm finally trying with a woman again, but slowly, with care, after two years trying to keep Maggie away. I've chosen Elizabeth in part for the modesty of her pace. She put Trajan and me in the second bedroom, where I spent all of the first night, most of the second, some of the third, and after Maggie arrived all the fourth. And this: Elizabeth is a striking woman, tall and sturdy with a long face, a strong chin, an elegant straight nose, and skin as smooth and unblemished as ivory. And she has a bit of prim American Gothic. She pulls her hair back around her head, drops it down in a long, thick, woven braid, loose but neat. She wears blouses under woolen jumpers and high-lacing country boots. Though not sensual or alluring or broadly open like Maggie, Elizabeth has my attention, perhaps for opposite reasons. Dark-skinned Maggie gets your attention with her eyes. She touches you and hugs you and pulls you into her before your time, and you love it, you love her body being close, you feel attractive, you return her touch and want more of her right away. Elizabeth is quiet pride and self-assurance and serenity like an old-fashioned churchgoer who has reaped the benefits of an active inner life, but there are hints of slumbering passion when she looks at me. She's a woman to be privately known, a prospect that suits me fine.

When Maggie showed up unannounced in Moscow, she brought Elizabeth and me to an abrupt halt. She came from her home in Ashland, Oregon on an out of the way route to Seattle and back, hoping, she said, to find her old friend and neighbor from the J Street house in Arcata, where Trajan and I still live. She had heard Elizabeth might be in Moscow, and there might be a couch for her. A plausible story for a vagabond like Maggie. She looked surprised to find Trajan and me there, but I know better. Elizabeth does, too.   And the friendship thing needs some correction. Maggie and Elizabeth were casual next-door neighbors, never close. Nor have they kept in touch. The real friendship has always been Elizabeth's and mine.

No, Maggie joined us by design, I'm sure. She phoned me from Ashland and heard my recorded message. She read between the lines. That's what brought her to Moscow.

WHEN MAGGIE AND I were hosting Arcata's version of the New Age on J Street, Elizabeth and her college roommates had Maggie's standing invitation to join in our too-frequent gatherings. She often accepted but rarely stayed long. Like me, Elizabeth only half-participated in the communalism being attempted all around us. The community garden and greenhouse in the backyard, the hot tub on our enclosed redwood deck (where she would not get naked), the crowded dinners at our kitchen table. Sometimes we would withdraw to her little front porch and redwood chairs and talk about what was or was not taking shape next door. We took a platonic interest in each other, and she, I believe, a careful savior's interest in me. She made herself available for intelligent conversation and friendship but made no overtures toward anything more. Nor did I, though I thought about it. We stayed on the edges of the New Age, enjoying its sociability, optimism and good feelings but not its lack of limits and privacy, edging closer to each other than to it, while Maggie immersed herself and left us behind.

Even before Trajan's birth, I began escaping more often to Elizabeth and her roommates and their quieter ways, the bluegrass music they played with friends in their living room, the stories of backpacking and tree planting, the crab feeds and sea songs. Their times with others were much briefer than ours, with greater spaces in between. Elizabeth and I came to depend on each other for a certain amount of attention. Maggie saw this, and the distance between us grew, but that did not propel Elizabeth and me into romance. I became too busy with Trajan, and Elizabeth would never let such a thing happen. With no problem we stayed in friendship, keeping our visits as infrequent as possible for the sake of a marriage and, later, a child. A silent understanding grew between us.

Once, after the conversation at the crowded table Maggie and I all too often presided over turned toward dreams of building a communal farm in the country, Elizabeth found me sitting alone on her porch, staring down J Street into a neighbor's cypress that dwarfs our houses. To my surprise, she had lingered at the table a bit longer than I had. Now she scooted a chair next to mine and seated herself less formally than was her custom, another surprise.

"I was raised on a farm," she said earnestly. "They should talk with me or my mother and father before they dream like that. They should read history. Human nature gets in the way of utopian dreams. Besides, the people at that table are city folk."

"It's an interesting abstraction, but I'm too private. It would be like more of what I've got too much of already."

Elizabeth stared at me and held it longer than she ever had. She breathed a deep sigh and rose from her chair. "Pardon me for saying this, but I think you need some time for yourself and some space for you and Maggie. Your baby is a month or so away."

"Thanks for seeing that."

"It's plain as day." She opened her front door, rushed in, and left me there.

BEFORE BED THAT NIGHT I spoke with Maggie in the kitchen. The crowd had shrunk to two dwelling on our living room floor. Maggie kept her back to me as she wiped the table and the counters.

"I get the feeling if I want more of your attention I must..." I waved my hand toward the door to the living room. "Pay more attention to all of this."

"That's right," Maggie said stiffly. "That would help you with me."

"Maggie, our home is a madhouse. I need some quiet here and some time with just you."

"It seems you're doing pretty well without me," she said, and headed for the stairs.

A month later Trajan was born at home. Everyone watched, except Elizabeth.

EVEN MAGGIE'S LEAVING for Ashland two years ago after our first and last big fight didn't draw Elizabeth and me together. After each visit on her front porch we would go our separate ways, unsure of what we wanted, of what was right. And if we had kindled a romance, Maggie's habit of coming back so often would have interfered. Elizabeth couldn't have liked that prospect. But in the weeks before she left for Moscow and graduate school six months ago, we began slow, shrinking circles around each other. Perhaps Moscow seemed far enough away from Maggie.

I helped her pack during the last few days. When we began talking about leaving some of her things with me, sentiment began to color our conversations.

"Take care of yourself," she said on the last moment of the last day. We were standing by her van. "And Trajan."

"I will." Then, veiled as an afterthought, "I'm going to miss you."

"Me, too. Visit my roommates. Sing with them."

"I should have done more of that these last months. I hardly know them."

"*We* should have." She folded her arms and rocked back and forth. "They won't bite."

"They aren't you."

She smiled and averted her eyes. "I'll call about my things."

We hugged from a distance, kissed each other on the cheek, and said goodbye.

She returned twice to collect her modest belongings - her long country dresses and a few simple pieces of furniture, her wooden and cast iron kitchen things, her second fiddle. Though she stayed with her old roommates, she spent most of her time with me. We began to look at each other differently, hugging and giving light kisses on our lips.

"Would you come visit me with Trajan?" she asked.

"Yes, I would do that."

In restrained letters and awkward phone calls we planned this visit, this now aborted beginning to something that may never come to pass.

THREE DAYS INTO THE VISIT, Elizabeth's front door opens. Maggie is standing there red-faced and cold, with lazy snowflakes floating in around her. Elizabeth looks first for Trajan's eyes, then mine. In my mind I record her chosen order as positive and important.

"Mama's here!" Trajan shouts. He runs to her, and she bends to catch him.

"Maggie, come in," Elizabeth says with forced conviction.

"I'm going to Seattle sort of round about," Maggie says when she's inside and has put Trajan down. Elizabeth closes the door and stands flushed beside it, behind her unwanted guest. Maggie glides to the couch and Trajan follows, attached to the back of her coat. They fall to the cushions and share grand hugs until Maggie stretches over him to take off her boots.

"I got a ride coming this way, so I thought I'd see how you're doing, Liz. And what a treat, my very own little man Trajan. Jack, what can I say?"

Her boots and socks are off, her high-arched little feet are pink with cold, her toes are wiggling. She leans back on the couch and draws our boy into another cuddle. He is smiling.

"Stay with us," Elizabeth says. Her unconvincing enthusiasm raises Maggie's eyebrows. "We'll find room for you on the floor."

I say to Trajan, "You're a lucky boy." I am still looking at Maggie's feet. They are so pretty.

THIS IS NOT MAGGIE'S FIRST DROP-IN during the last two years. Three or four times a year she takes a "timeout," she calls it, "from the intensity of my life to the quiet of yours." A capitulation that has gratified me more than I wish to admit. Rarely has she given even a day's notice, and never is she derailed by the implications for Trajan of how often these visits happen. She rests, nests, cleans, preens like a cat, and mothers like it's all she knows. She tries to find her way into my bed, and she gets there. I'm not proud of this, but it's still delicious.

One morning after she surprised me at nearly midnight, Trajan found us in bed. He climbed in between us, pulled us close, and kept us there for half an hour. His big round eyes floated back and forth between us, then wandered on the ceiling.

"This has got to stop," I said when Trajan left for the bathroom.

"He shouldn't see love and feel it?"

"This isn't love, Maggie, but we won't get into that. I'm going to try harder to stop this." I got up and started dressing. Maggie watched and didn't answer.

WITHOUT A WORD, Elizabeth and I drop the original script, though we never knew what it was. For two days we try to settle for nods, touches on elbows, quick brushes of hands. When we can, we stand at the kitchen counter and try to become attached at the hip, hoping Maggie will take notice. With sighs through tightened lips, we tell each other we're wondering what might have been and will there be another time?

Before Trajan awakens late Sunday morning, when he and I are to leave, Maggie announces she needs to go home. She does not mention Seattle, nor does she ask for a ride. It's a given. Ashland is on an easy route to Arcata.

"What happened to Seattle?" I ask her.

"It's a mother thing." She is sitting cross-legged on the couch, examining her fingers. "We need this time."

She's right, but I hate the way she went about it. I hear something else. I hear that "we" includes me, and I suspect that before we get to Ashland Maggie will imply the usual possibilities. Eschewing settling for less, I sit on the arm of Elizabeth's chair and caress her neck and shoulders. They are stiff as bands of wire.

"I'll have no time to stay there," I say. "It's a work thing."

Maggie stares at us. Elizabeth's hand finds its way to my knee.

"Trajan could stay with me for a few days," Maggie says. "Or I could come down to the coast."

I rise and pull Elizabeth up with me and give her a full-bodied hug. I feel a little guilty about this, but words are not enough for Maggie.

"We'll talk about that later," I say.

Elizabeth obliges me with a kiss on the cheek. With Trajan out of harm's way, she is playing the game for me. I love it. I hate it.

"I'll take a shower now, Elizabeth," Maggie says, "if you don't mind."

"Of course, Maggie. You needn't ask."

Elizabeth and I pull each other close and linger over a kiss. I relish her abandonment of decorum. Her body feels good, her strong pull a declaration I want to believe. Maggie's footsteps pound on the stairs. When Elizabeth and I let go, our faces are red with embarrassed smiles.

MAGGIE'S SHOWER is interminably long. The change that has come over Elizabeth and me has made me less inclined to hurry. A big brunch stretches through a languid afternoon for two pairs that work hard to stay in separate rooms, Maggie and Trajan in the living room, Elizabeth and I in the kitchen. We have trouble avoiding each other and seem to want each other in the impatient way of new lovers who know their time is running out. No door separates the two rooms, and either bedroom is out of the question. By midafternoon we are frustrated, and I am anxious to be done with this, to be home with Trajan or, if necessary, without him. From a few whispered words I know that Elizabeth understands and agrees. We take a long last walk in the snow, stopping at a deli for food for the road, sharing cold kisses and stiff hugs, and avoiding talk of Maggie or the future.

At the door she unzips her overcoat and my down jacket and pulls me into a hug, her body snug against mine, her arms around my back, her chin buried against my neck.

"Would Maggie always be a problem?"

"She's difficult."

"Trajan needs her. Do you need her?"

When I don't answer, she pulls away. "Please think about that. I like you, I really do, but I need that question answered." When she opens the door and pulls me in, I can see her constructing a polite smile. A sense of hurry pervades the half hour we need to pack, fill our cooler, and exchange our awkward goodbyes.

For the first several hours, we are mostly quiet, and I decide to think only about Trajan. He has hardly let go of Maggie since she opened Elizabeth's door. This is not what I had in mind, but I have not been able to resist watching him cuddling in her arms, or walking with her and holding her hand, or laughing and playing in the snow. They look so good together. Maggie does that part right, when she does it.

JACKRABBITS AS BIG as good-sized dogs jump out of the darkness and freeze in the headlights, almost assuring a bad result. They start one way, then go the other, and some switch back again. I try to avoid them by crossing the centerline and bumping the shoulder. Nearly half don't make it. When almost ten go down in five hours, I stop dodging and counting. If I go straight ahead, their odds are just as good, and we are safer.

"Straight ahead," I whisper when the next one appears.

"You've been aiming for them," Maggie accuses. "It's so unlike you."

"If I were aiming for them, I'd move where they move, and I'd have better results."

"You're trying to irritate me because I showed up at Elizabeth's. Can't you just say it?"

I feel her hot stare on the side of my face, but a hint of a cry hides in her voice.

"I can convince you it was an accident," she says.

"I'm trying to save gas. Straight ahead saves gas."

"If you had thought of that sooner, we'd get to a real bed in Klamath Falls."

I'm certain she wants a double bed for us and a rollaway for Trajan. It's the old formula that keeps us bound. Constant tension and handy triggers like Big Ugly E and the rabbits equals fighting and forgiving, equals tears and hugs, equals grand, voracious, consuming, insatiable sex. We know how it works, and all the ingredients are in place.

"I haven't swerved enough to make a difference."

"If you had gotten gas in John Day, we would make it to my bed in Ashland."

"No *we* wouldn't."

"I mean Trajan and I."

"Say what you mean."

"You like her, don't you?"

I think of Trajan and remain silent.

"Are you going to answer that?"

"Not in present company."

"Trajan's asleep."

I look at her. "Not for long, the way you're going."

"You could nod."

"We traveled fourteen hours to visit her. We had five days. Think about it."

"You two were putting on an act for me. You're not serious about each other."

"We're going to stay in Cumby. In the car, in the cold. By a pump at a closed gas station."

"At your seventy-five we run out of gas. At my fifty-five we get there safely."

Trajan stirs. His eyes open to narrow slits. He isn't smiling.

"Cumby will be too small for a gas station," she says.

"Make one of your positive affirmations and go to sleep. I'll stay in my lane."

Maggie falls silent, which suits me. The fight that hovers beneath our surfaces would awaken Trajan. I hear his clogged little nose and see her chin on the fur of his hood, making a different picture than I had wanted for this trip, but good enough to protect, to make into a memory that will serve him. If she and I keep it together.

We drive on. Trajan awakens and stays that way more now than not, dozing and coming back. He is trying to not miss much, to figure everything out and keep the spirit of adventure. If his mother weren't here, I would make Big Ugly E a treasure he would never forget. Instead the night is an ordeal for me and a quandary for him. I promise myself to keep the peace.

His slow deep breathing soothes me. He watches me. I switch from defrost to heat and slow to fifty-five.

TEN MINUTES LATER the needle centers perfectly over Big Ugly E. I figure we are twenty miles from Cumby.

Maggie leans over to see. "Is it grim?"

"We might make it," I say, hoping to change the energy.

Trajan starts us dreaming. "Cumby's gonna have a gas station!"

"It will be warm, and the bathrooms will be clean," says Maggie, trying for enthusiasm. She looks at me for acknowledgement.

"At 2:00 a.m. a fresh pot of coffee will sit on the counter," I say, returning her tentative smile.

"And hot chocolate with marshmallows and whipped cream," says Trajan.

"And herb tea in little bags and boiling water."

"The hot chocolate, yes," I say. "But the herb tea? Not in Cumby."

Maggie arches her back and sighs. "Party pooper," she whispers a laugh with that deep, throaty resonance that makes me want her right through my anger. Her eyes catch the lights of the dashboard.

I glower at her without real disapproval. "Isn't the pot calling the kettle black?"

"We'll pass on that."

"Why did the pot call the kettle black?" Trajan asks.

"We'll pass on that, too," Maggie says. "Until we're

not so tired and cranky. Okay, little man?"

Trajan looks back and forth between us. A smile begins at his mouth and travels all over his face, lighting up his eyes. He has our attention. He is in the middle of us, where he wants to be.

"Let's pretend we get exactly what we want at Cumby," I say. "Me - a gas pump and decent coffee; Trajan - hot chocolate; Maggie - warmth, clean bathrooms, even hot tea."

"How far will it be to Klamath Falls?" Maggie asks. "I could drive."

"Maggie, no one will be up."

"Weren't we trying to think positively?"

"Getting to Cumby will be positive enough."

I fix my vision on the spot where the centerline disappears. Maggie turns her face away. Trajan twists around to face forward. I wonder if this is still an adventure for him.

A NAME ON A MAP can mean as little as a hand painted wooden sign next to a general store beside a lineless county road. I remember such a sign beside a C-shaped arrangement of three vine-covered school buses, but there was no pump. I do see a rusty pump when I pass the town of Wonder, Oregon in the mountains between Ashland and Arcata. Wonder consists of a run-down house, an octagonal geodesic dome, a teepee, a well, and behind the pump, a store that's always "Shut." Wonder has a sign, and its name is on the map.

There have been towns on maps I couldn't find on the road. I wish I had taken the Cumby route on the trip to Moscow. Then I would know.

We get quiet. Trajan squeezes tighter into Maggie and falls back into sleep. The fog of our collective breathing begins to win the battle for the windshield. I turn the heat back to defrost and lean forward to stretch my stiff back and shake out the heaviness in my head. The jackrabbits are no longer hopping onto the road. They are sleeping.

I worry alone.

A SPOT OF WHITE NEON appears in the distance and grows larger. Red letters take shape in a blue border. A possible gas station. I squint until "Metro Natural Gas and Propane" comes into focus. Not a gas station, but maybe there will be a pump for trucks and a Good Samaritan. I slow down along a high chain link fence topped with barbed wire. The right shoulder widens, and a gate opens to a gravel yard bordered by two huge warehouses that my lights sweep as I turn through the gate. In between them sits a small house with a covered front porch. No lights are on in the house, or atop a dozen tall poles on the edges of the empty lot.

The change in speed and the crunch of gravel awaken Maggie and Trajan.

"What on earth are you doing?" Maggie asks.

"Looking for a pump and signs of life. Some good old country man is going to wake up and help us out of this jam." I downshift to first gear and ease toward the little house, looking left and right.

"A pump, maybe, but anything alive will be sleeping. You will wake it up, and it will be mad."

"I thought you were a master of positive expectations. Ask and you shall receive. That sort of thing."

I'm glad Maggie doesn't respond. At the far end of the larger building on the right, a red-boarded windowless thing, sits a single pump. Diesel probably, I say to myself, but it's worth a try. I let the car roll to a stop along the house, but keep it running.

"You've lost it," she says.

"What's Daddy lost, Mama?" I detect a hint of fear.

"Jack, this doesn't feel right," she says, peering at the little house. Trajan nuzzles into her and keeps his eyes on me. "Daddy hasn't lost anything, little man. I just disagree with him. Jack, let's get out of here."

Just as I decide to oblige her, the yard lights burst on with repetitive pops like Fourth of July fireworks. I swallow hard and imagine the gate closing in front of us, warning shots overhead, flashing police lights speeding in our direction, a harsh siren. I ease into first gear, hoping not to waste gas or add to Trajan's fright. I give him a little smile and let it stay on my face for Maggie to see. In the rearview mirror I see the house's door open and a man stride off the porch. In second gear I feel the crunch of rocks under wheels, the sudden shift to pavement, and acceleration matching my heartbeat.

Their eyes stay on me all the way through fifth gear. We are a quarter of a mile down the road before Maggie breaks the silence with her soft, rusty voice. "What a rush!" She snickers from deep in her throat. I watch her shaking the tension from her hands. I never expected to share any more rushes with Maggie, save for those that I fail to avoid in bed.

"Watch the road, Jack." Her eyes are as soft as her voice. A smile breaks across her lips, an immeasurable blend of amusement and appreciation. Always a chameleon, I think. I wonder if Elizabeth has as many colors and shades.

Trajan straightens up. "Yeah, Dad, watch the road!"

"Now let's see about Cumby, Jack. How much farther?"

"Maybe ten miles. I predict a slumbering pump."

"What's that, Dad?"

"A sleeping pump."

"You mean no one's awake there!" he shouts. "What will we do?"

"We'll improvise."

"You're confusing him, Jack."

"Trajan, that means we have to wait and see what we need to do."

He looks back and forth between us, then lays his head against Maggie's shoulder and breathes in. His eyes remain wide open.

Big Ugly E stands uncovered by the needle. A pale glow illuminates a capitalized bright red word on the dashboard. FUEL. I can feel Maggie's eyes on the side of my face and see her hand, ungloved now, very close to the edge of my seat, fingers curled upward, inviting. I think to put my hand in hers, to entwine our fingers, but I don't.

WE WATCH BIG UGLY E the rest of the way to Cumby. Cumby is a gas station with a single pump, a little house not more than ten yards away, a plastic bar called The High

Desert Tap behind an over-sized parking lot, and a market and restaurant crowding the other side of the road.   No lights are on inside or out. I pull up to the pump and edge the tank port up to Unleaded Regular. I get out, stretch, run two laps around the car and the pump, get the bags and a blanket from the trunk, and throw them into the backseat.

"Put more layers on. This is home for the night. Maggie, put my Easy Rider sweater on Trajan." I think to myself, we may have saved his adventure.

"This must be a new acquisition," Maggie says.

"You do remember Jack Nicholson's Ole Miss letter sweater in the movie? He wore it when he rode the motorcycle. Trajan's been our easy rider."

"That's not exactly encouraging. What happened to the Jack in the movie almost happened to this Jack and us a few minutes ago."

"That's a stretch," I say. "Let's drop it." I'm irritated again, this time at the wrong turn of an innocent remark. Trajan doesn't need to hear the details of a movie in which a man wearing a sweater like the one he's putting on gets blasted off a motorcycle.

When I get in the car, Maggie shifts toward the center and lays her hand on my shoulder. She strokes it gently. Trajan never says a word, as if he senses that this is something between adults. I wink at him, try a slight smile, and get a little one back.

"Tomorrow's Sunday, Jack," Maggie says. "This place won't open early."

"Someone who works here will see us. At sunup that someone will awaken us with a knock on the window and ask what we want. I'll tell him to fill 'er up. We'll be in Klamath Falls before the church folks get to the Denny's. Our bodies will hurt and we'll be exhausted, but at least there'll be a Denny's, maybe something better. That's the way it's going to be."

"Maybe we'll find a health food restaurant," says Maggie.

"Whichever comes first. That's likely to be a Denny's."

"Ooookay," she says, removing her hand from my shoulder. "Whatever you say, Jack."

WE GET QUIET after a bumping rush to add layers. To my amazement, Maggie keeps Trajan on her lap, and some sleep actually happens. When Elizabeth appears at the edges of mine, I try to push her in front of Maggie. As I drift off, this becomes a pleasant little game, approaching delicious. I hear the engine choke to a stop and have the wherewithal to turn off the ignition. There are a few groans and some shifting around. I learn a few things: a watched clock hardly moves; the old Toyota's windows are even less sealed than I thought - air seeps through them even when the car is still; Maggie has developed a low, wheezy snore that I find attractive; I still enjoy watching her sleep, the way her shuttered eyes flutter, the involuntary movements of her full lips; Trajan looks so damn good with her, which I already knew, which I miss right through the acceptance of this split that will not heal, that we do not let heal; and on a cold night everything natural to a desert sleeps more easily than its accidental guests.

Not many sounds break the silence until the sun comes up behind us. The first sound and the second and the third are trucks, eighteen-wheelers that shake us and stir us awake, but most of the time we sleep until the sun is high enough to brighten the sky.

THREE TAPS ON THE WINDOW. I straighten up and shake my residents before I turn. I want them to see this. With my left hand I crank the window down halfway.

A young woman peers over a scarf that barely shows the tip of her nose. She surveys the scene, pulls down the scarf, and shakes her head.

"Good morning there," she finally says. "What for you?"

"Fill 'er up."

"That'll be regular?"

"Yes ma'am."

She nods, readjusts her scarf, looks at us for a few more seconds, and backs away, staring. Maggie grins.

I scan my passengers, waiting with conceit for expected congratulations. Maggie's grin becomes a chuckle that wants to become a laugh. Trajan mumbles into Maggie's coat. "I knew everything was gonna be okay," he says.

"Is this a pit stop for anyone?" I ask.

Trajan asks, "What's a pit stop?"

"The heater, please," Maggie says.

"It's illegal to run the engine during fill-up. How about a well-deserved round of applause for the fortune teller?"

"What's illegal?" Trajan asks.

"Not now, Trajan," I say. "I'll explain at breakfast. A pit stop is a timeout to go to the bathroom."

We fall silent again and wait. At three more taps on the window, I turn and roll it back down.

"Ten bucks," she says. "I stopped at ten so's I don't have to give you change in this cold. What else for you?"

I find a ten in my wallet and pass it through the window.

"How far to Klamath Falls?"

She points to a sign not fifty feet away.

"Thirty-four, I suppose," she says. "Restaurant here opens in an hour, but in Klamath there's a Denny's always open this side of town."

"How'd you know we wanted to hear about breakfast?"

She scratches her head above an earmuff. "You wouldn't understand. Sort of a psychic power comes over people out here long about this time of the morning, about twelve hours after dinner."

I nod thoughtfully. "Thanks," I say. "I'll remember that. Do we owe you any rent?"

She snorts and waves me off. "Go on outta here. You're frostin' your folks and me, too." She turns toward the store. I watch her shaking her head all the way inside.

We are quiet for the two or three minutes it takes the defroster to clear the windows. At first I watch the needle creep away from Big Ugly E, then my passengers warming up. Maggie tries to stretch her legs. Trajan hardly moves. He purrs through his nose, and his eyelids try to flutter off the weight of sleep. From above him comes a lovely, deep-throated, womanly groan, a melody for a morning, the kind I miss and am not certain Elizabeth can provide, a salutation to the day that says its maker has forgotten the difficult night, the last four days, and the role she played. I have mostly liked that about Maggie. For her it's over when it's over. The problem is, when you forget so easily, how can you reflect, reconsider, or think about the consequences, or change? As always though, Maggie has managed to garner the benefit of my doubt. She leans toward me, lays her hand on my thigh, and chuckles deep in her throat.

"What a night," she says.

I want to say we should have left at noon, but that would tell Trajan the adventure wasn't worth it. Or I could say, "What a vacation" or "What a wonderful coincidence that you showed up in Moscow." But I don't.

"Sure was," I say. "It's a kick to race the needle, isn't it, Trajan? I guess we won."

"You mean this was fun, right?"

"Yep, that's what I mean."

He sits up proudly. "You sure were right about everything!" he announces. "It happened *just* like you said."

"You're too lucky," Maggie says. "I would like to be that lucky."

"This was your luck, too. Isn't it enough for one day?"

She looks at me with pursed lips and a steady gaze, concealing something I would like to see, a smile or a frown or a question. Trajan scrambles to the backseat and sits himself right in the middle, up close.

"I don't know. Do I need more luck?"

I pull away from the pump and turn onto the highway, looking mostly straight ahead. Maggie removes her hand from my thigh. I try to see Elizabeth in front of me. She comes and she goes, and in between is Maggie. The mountains beyond Klamath Falls rise green above the desert, bright in the morning sun. Further still is Ashland, then Arcata way down on the coast. We have a long way to go.

THAT GIRL

STANDING AT THE KITCHEN SINK with her hands in warm dishwater, Ella gazes out the window toward the sun setting right at the spot where the street curves into leafless trees. She counts down six houses on the left to her ex-husband's place and wonders whether her Lucinda is there or somewhere on the street. Lamont is sitting behind her at the kitchen table, his first place of rest every night after pushing a broom and a mop, or on the worst days, wrestling a waxing machine down long corridors. Any second now, his questions will start. Lamont has grilled Ella from that chair about her daughter's troubles almost every night of the year he has stayed with her. Always at dinnertime, while Ella cooks. She can feel him staring.

"Finally off my feet," he growls.

Ella wants to say she never gets off hers till after her cleaning job *and* making dinner, but she doesn't. When she fusses with Lamont before he mellows, his dark mood gets darker, his questions harder.

She scrubs a pot, muffles a grunt, and watches a car turn in front of the straight, dark trunks and splintered shafts of light, then pass out of sight. For the last four months, since her fifteen-year-old left for her father's, Lamont's questions have felt more like hard rain than drizzle.

"What you laughin' at?" Lamont asks.

"Oh, just a thought passin'. Nothing about you."

Lamont takes off his boots and throws them into the corner behind the table. He stretches against the wooden chair until its joints creak in protest and yawns bigger than any man she knows. When his questions don't begin right away, Ella figures Lamont has picked up something about Lucinda from the talk in the neighborhood. He catches up with most of what she hasn't told him. Four months ago she didn't tell him that Lucinda would be staying with her father, but someone else did. A month before, that Lucinda was pregnant, but the gossip about that reached him, too. No point giving Lamont bad news about Lucinda, she thinks, he going to find out anyway, and his questions be flying.

Ella washes each dish in near slow motion, never turning to face him. She stares down the road toward the weak light of the lowering winter sun and tries to imagine Lucinda in William's house, though she reckons her daughter is anywhere but there. Her thoughts run to nights Lamont has come home with news she had not given him.

"He babies that girl worse than you," Lamont had said when he had discovered that Ella agreed to let Lucinda go to her father's. "She stay with that playboy, she gonna flunk eighth grade worse than last time."

It didn't take long for Ella to agree. On the phone Lucinda kept saying how much easier life was at her father's. Then she stopped calling. When Ella called, Lucinda often wasn't there. Sometimes William didn't know where she was, and Darlene, the new wife, didn't seem to care. William wouldn't admit this, but Ella knew. And she knew that Lucinda was no better off.

"Wouldn't a happened if you had control," Lamont had said a month ago when he came home with the news that Lucinda was pregnant. "I shoulda harped on you *every*day."

"You don't?" Ella had asked with a turn and a glare.

"Not enough on a woman who don't listen."

Tonight Lamont is too quiet. The newest bad news must have reached him.

"You a snoopin' bear," she says to the window, then counts houses again. In the near-darkness William's place is only lights.

"I ain't a bear, and I ain't snoopin'."

Ella forces a nod and plunges a skillet into the water.

"Don't have to snoop," Lamont continues. "Everything come around."

"You goin' to tell me what you heard on the bus this time?"

"I shouldn't have to find out about Lucinda's dumbshit crap on the bus."

Ella bites her lip and nods ever so slightly. It's coming, she thinks, it's coming. She withdraws her hands from the water and dries them with a dishtowel, one finger at a time. The light outside is only a thin band at the base of the trees.

"What you noddin' at?" Lamont asks.

"Just gettin' ready for what's comin'."

"Nothing you don't bring on yourself. Tell me why you won't tell me nothing."

Ella twists around to nearly face him. "You heard me say a thousand times I hope William do better. He got a woman staying home."

"That woman don't come home every night like I do." Lamont shifts in his chair and clasps his huge hands behind his neck.

Ella turns back to the sink and starts to wipe down its edges. "What we was doin' worth about nothing."

"What I was doin's what you mean. That why you sent her off? That and the GED you been trying for since whenever?" He looks away from her.

"Lucinda been gone four months and now you ask about the GED?" Ella knows there is truth to his words, but she is surprised by Lamont's new line of attack. "I woulda started for that diploma long time ago if everything fine right here. Then community college."

"How many times you gonna let that girl fuck up you goin' back to school? Three? Four?"

"That girl has a name, and twice is all." Ella goes to the stove and pushes her hips into its warmth. "Why you all of a sudden so interested in me goin' back to school?"

Lamont looks down at his hands. One is a fist the other keeps rubbing.

"Tell me why," Ella says.

"Don't know," he mutters. "Make us more money. Make you happy. Whatever."

Ella sighs. "Some timing' you got."

"What you mean by that?"

"A baby comin' make everything different."

"Uhhuh," Lamont grunts softly like he does when he doesn't want to admit that he agrees. "In May?" he asks.

Ella stretches to the sink for a sponge and begins to wipe the stove's shiny surface. "Good guess, for a man. Late May."

Lamont shifts in his chair. "When Lucinda comin' back?"

"You never seen me make something happen so quick," Ella answers. "No other woman raisin' my grandbaby."

"You givin' up on the GED?"

"You think I goin' to leave a baby and a new mama without a lick of sense with you most every night?"

Lamont looks up at her with eyes round and wide. "You a hard woman."

"What can you teach Lucinda about a baby?"

He looks back down at his hands. "You really hard."

Ella scrubs at a tiny spot near the back of the stove. She hears fingers drumming on the tabletop, then chair legs squeaking on linoleum.

"I smell roast." Lamont says. "Since when we can afford roast?"

"I got to do something to feel better."

"What else on the menu?"

Smiling to herself, Ella bends to peek into the oven. Lamont can't stay bothered about anything when food is on his mind and its smell in his nose. He backing off, she thinks. One of us always do when the words strike close.

"Menu! Potatoes, gravy, butter beans, stuff you like," she answers. "Next you goin' to ask me what you did to deserve it." She knows he is staring and imagines two beams of heat piercing her back.

"I heard about Lucinda today," he says. "Why you always hold that stuff from me?"

Finally, Ella thinks. She moves back to the window to watch the last light. She reaches into the water for the last pot, finds the sponge, and begins to scrub again. The rows of small, tired houses glow softly, and for a moment everything looks more right than it is. Only the warm water on her hands and the hot oven three feet away keep Ella from going out into the cold for that fooling light. She chuckles, puts her hands in the dishwater, and closes her eyes.

"I askin' you somethin'!" Lamont yells like he would at Lucinda. "And what you do? Laugh at me like I'm a fool."

"I'm laughin' at life." Her voice is almost a whisper. "It put real different things on top of you at the same time. Let you down and push you up, then back down."

"Answer me, dammit!" He raises a fist as if to strike the table, but it comes down easy, like always. "Answer my damn question 'stead of starin' out that window thinkin' about whatever. I askin' you something."

Ella turns and walks to the other end of the table.

"Why don't you tell me what you heard?" she asks, her voice even quieter. "Let me see if you got it right."

"Damn, you still duckin' my question!"

Ella sits, takes in a deep breath. It's time, she thinks, it's time. She folds her hands on the table. "You got one way with Lucinda. Yellin'. Like now." Her fingers rub at her lower lip and chin like she is trying to pull out the words. "Not tellin' you things, that's how I keep you off her. She don't need you for a diet."

Lamont looks down at the table, then back to Ella. "That why you sent her off?"

"Your way do no good for a troubled child," she says. "I won't feed it."

"You never said it like that before." His eyes seem smaller, little lost ships looking for a place to land.

Ella grabs the edge of the table, stares, waits.

"The GED thing got nothin' to do with it?" Lamont asks.

"I won't say that."

"And now she comin' back pregnant and no sense to raise a child. That girl gonna keep you out of school forever."

"You the only one talkin' about school." Ella lets go of the table, laces her fingers, and rests her hands on its surface.

"This the most I ever got from you." Lamont stares right at her. "But you still not tellin' me what else goin' on with that girl. I know what it is, but you got to tell me."

"She has a name you can use."

"Woman, you sure drive a hard bargain." He is almost smiling, and his thick shoulders slump. "You a mule."

Ella knows he will stop pushing now. She glances over her shoulder at the clock above the stove. "Buttin' against one mule too hard for the other?"

Lamont grumbles a laugh and flashes the toothiest smile she can remember in the year they've been together.

She straightens in the chair and crosses her arms against her stomach. "Lucinda want to raise her child with Beatrice." She snorts a laugh that reminds her of Lamont when he can't believe something. "Fifteen-year-old thinkin' she can raise her baby with a girlfriend who just as bad off." She lets her shoulders sag and her arms fall into her lap. "She hangin' with some mama girls in Few Gardens. Those project girls use welfare to buy for theyselves, and they boyfriends pushin' drugs." She shifts in her chair. "Lucinda and Beatrice lookin' for a place there, and it gets worse. Beatrice want to have a child, too, and don't care who with. Just like Lucinda."

"They gonna make the cutest family."

"You think I like tellin' this stuff to a yellin' man?"

"When you quit your hardness, woman?" His voice is quiet, nearly soft.

"When you quit yours."

Lamont lets out a breath and crosses his arms like he's hugging himself. "What else you got to tell me?"

"That I need to be here for the baby till I see what little mama be like." Ella pauses and smiles. "And what you be like."

Lamont tries a gruff look, but it fails. "She gonna fuss big time about not goin' off with Beatrice."

"Fussin's fine, but goin' be over my dead body."

"Mine, too."

"You best let me do the nasty work." Ella can't resist a grin, but she shrinks it. "Can you try somethin' beside that hammer you always swingin'?"

"That what it is?"

"To Lucinda."

Lamont looks right at Ella. "She say that?"

"Things like it."

Ella props her elbows on the table, rests her chin on folded hands, and stares toward the window and the flat darkness outside. She closes her eyes.

"My little girl dreamin' the mother dream, just like I did. She has no idea, same as I didn't. Till she do, someone got to give her child a world to like."

"What she gonna give?"

"Some things come natural. The rest her mama got to show her."

Ella looks at Lamont staring down at the table. He seems to be thinking hard at something, she hopes at what it takes to raise a child or, better yet, a child and its mother. His chin rests on fingers laced together, not on fists poised for another strike that wouldn't happen. Maybe this time, she thinks, his own self is heavy on his mind.

He raises his head, and his eyes meet hers. "You really want to go to school, don't you?"

"Someday. But now's my teachin' time, not my learnin' time."

Lamont rises, arches his back until his belly shows beneath his tee shirt, and crosses to the stove in two huge steps.

"That roast ready?" he asks without looking back.

Ella smiles broadly and chuckles.

"What you laughin' at?"

"First time I remember you puttin' off food this long for talkin'."

Lamont bends, opens the oven door, and sniffs at the narrow opening.

"Smells good and cooked. Must be ready."

"You got to take a knife to it."

He eases the door shut, and Ella smiles again. She can't remember him not letting it slam. He turns and leans against the oven's warmth. His hands look lost until they find the edge of the stove behind him.

Ella pushes herself up and ambles to the top drawer by the refrigerator. She fishes for a knife heavy and sharp enough to slice the roast, tests the blade with her fingers, chooses a fork, and turns to face him.

"Be careful," she says as she hands them to him. Her eyes are wide open, searching.

Lamont's lips are drawn together in a firm line. He takes the knife and fork with gentler hands than she thought he had. They touch hers for what seems like an extra moment, but she's not certain. After a split-second nod, he turns to the oven.

Ella lingers for a second, close to Lamont, then back-steps to the window and turns to stare into the darkness. With so many windows lit up, she can't count down six houses, but she can almost see the road bending away, into the trees.

HIGHWAY 47

GREY PULLED OFF THE ROAD in a meadowed valley to stretch and watch the fading evening light. Beyond the narrow stretch of tall grass, hills dusted with early snow rose like rounded steps to higher and higher summits. He loved the land's brown curves, the lacing arms of bare trees reaching up, the creeks coming down through rocky draws, but it was too late for even the shortest hike up the beckoning gravel roads. He had been pushing himself all day, never getting out for more than a stretch. Getting home to Lesley before ten o'clock wasn't the only reason or even the main one. The rhythm of Highway 47's rolling turns had hooked him into a race against the clock, saving him from the familiar road dreams he had been trying to escape, leaving him content to soak up the dying light and dimming woods and hills in mesmerizing motion.

He jogged four circles around the car and tried a few perfunctory stretches before getting back in. Soon Highway 47 gave up the meadow for a forest tunnel, his high beams piercing it like a miner's light, his dashboard reflecting him back on himself from both side windows. He floated past lone houses and closed stores under pale fluorescent cautionary lights. Random scenes from within replaced the cold landscape, flashing by like a sped-up silent movie: Lesley sipping wine at the kitchen table, wondering how early he had left; his mother probing before he left, her nosiness trumping her caution; the week of work ahead, needing to be planned; a woman somewhere on the road, inviting him. Grey tried to follow that last one, but six hours with few stops had tired him. The images flooded by too fast until the perk from the last cup of coffee wore off, and the scenes began to fade. He blinked his eyes and forced them open with imaginary posts and beams, then clamps and vice-grips. He sermonized aloud on favored topics and worked out the logic of strong convictions. Anything to keep moving.

He surfed the radio: country western, talk show politics, weather reports from somewhere about snow, forgettable oldies, country western, fire and brimstone, talk show psychology, storm watches, country western, biblical prophecy, talk show politics, metallic rock and roll and rock and roll and on and on until a road sign announced his immediate goal, Payune, twenty miles. He relaxed and imagined a booth in Denny's with chinking dishes and steaming bad coffee, a newspaper, a breakfast plate.

The thought of food gave Grey a second wind. He shut off the unrelenting radio trash, cracked his window to an unexpected damp chill, and straightened up for the run to Payune. A dot of blue neon appeared where the road dissolved in the last strands of crimson daylight at the end of the tunnel of trees. The dot grew and took on shape, slid out of sight, came back over the road refined into "Adrian's Diner." He slowed and coasted toward a left turn into the parking lot. A road sign appeared in his headlights. "Payune 14." He thought about pushing on to predictable fast food. He might make it home before Lesley turned in, but his tired back and feet had already taken command. His stomach growled agreement. He took the left.

Adrian's Diner was a flat rectangular addition that ruined a cozy two-story, steep-peaked house of unpainted wood. The latter wore single windows on either side of a centered front door and a double above, tight under the peak. The diner was all windows with blinds drawn down and slats left open. Grey could see no one inside, but an "Open" sign hung in a pane of the front door. Overhead a thin veil of gray permitted the night's first stars to shine through, but the cold, damp hint of snow surprised him. He wished he had listened to the weather reports and thought again about moving on.

He wondered whether Adrian was a woman, and that possibility got him through the door. It opened to a tinkling of bells, soft like the wind chimes Lesley hung from the eaves by their back door a few years before. He stood for a moment in the diner's soft light and warm browns, so different from the white glare he had expected. On the window side of a wide aisle sat a row of booths, on the inside a counter with a row of stools. In a gap in the counter stood a small display case with an antique cash register mounted on its glass surface. Each booth had a beige and white-checkered tablecloth, dark brown vinyl benches, and a brassy little jukebox under the window. Above the jukes, light beige wall lamps with small cream-colored shades cast a row of downward glows. Even the blinds were milky brown. The slow, warm colors would keep him off the road a while. He figured Adrian's Diner for a mom and pop place run by friendly older folks. Oh well, he thought, they would know about the weather and, with luck, have a passable paper and serve breakfast at dinner with a decent cup of coffee.

Grey stood there, hands in his pockets, choosing his spot. A young boy he took for five or six came in from a door behind the left end of the counter. He watched the boy fill a water glass and take a set of utensils wrapped in a brown paper napkin from a drawer. Balancing the load in his little hands, the boy went to a window booth and arranged the setting with great care, looking resolute, important. Impressed, Grey gave a rather formal nod and held back the broad grin, then settled into the booth and took off his glasses to rub his eyes. The boy watched him, his shoulders relaxing out of his waiter pose. After a few seconds, he scurried around the counter and through the door behind it as if on his way to report the completion of an assignment. Propping his elbows on the table, Grey leaned his head into his hands to let the stiffness ease from his neck and shoulders.

When he shut his eyes, the road reappeared, taking him in and out of turns, up and down rises and falls. He felt his car turning into the diner's parking lot and saw a young woman peering through its bank of windows. A scraping sound, rubber boots on the floor, intruded. He looked up to see the boy at the edge of the booth, his face peering from the tightened furry hood of a winter coat. Their eyes met, Grey winked, and the boy, his waiter's demeanor now

abandoned, gave him a shy grin and scooted toward the
door, scraping the heels of his boots on the floor with each
step. Grey lay his head back in his hands, closed his eyes,
and found himself back in the driver's seat, opening the car
window to the chill air and hint of snow. I'll be really late
now, he thought, what with this break. He was tired and
knew it would be a long one.

He heard the door click shut, the bells hanging on it
mingling with the sound of a woman's voice, dusky and
pleasant.

"Can I help you?"

Startled, he straightened up with a jerk.

"Are you okay?" the waitress asked, her voice
cautious. She stared wide-eyed, her pupils bobbing around
in large, clear whites, her arms crossed in front of her.

"I'm all right, just tired," he said, looking up. An oval
nameplate bearing "Adrian" in cursive letters rode a field of
yellow leaves on long, brown stems. "And hungry."

"There are menus." She pointed at the jukebox at the
window end of the booth. The menus were behind it.
"Something to drink?"

He looked past her down the row of booths. Against
the wall at the far end of the diner's broad aisle sat a big
juke, brassy-brown and ruling. He noticed that the counter
had little jukes across from every third or fourth round,
brown vinyl stool.

Adrian stood there, waiting. "I'll just come back."

"I'm sorry. Such a nice place. Just water, thanks."

"Sure," she said, turning away.

"Haven't been in a jukebox diner in a long time. Nice
touch from the past. I'm really sorry. Falling asleep. I guess I
was more tired than I thought."

She nodded and motioned again to the menus. "I'll
give you a few minutes to order."

"Nice colors in here," he said.

"I like them."

"Every shade of brown."

"That's right."

"Well, I guess I should look this over."

"Good idea," she said, turning away. She's autumn,
Grey thought. Copper penny hair, freckled skin, reddish

brown eyes. She was lean and athletic with strong, high
shoulders and a small waist and firm, freckled arms that
matched her hair. He followed the loose braid down past her
waist to the curve of her yellow-leaved dress, then back up
to her arm as it stretched to clean the grill, revealing the
profile of her breast. Not until she glanced over her shoulder
did Grey finally reach for a menu, but the jukebox distracted
him. He scanned the songs. Adrian, sniffing at a coffee
maker and wiping down a broad grill, was difficult not to
look at. She glanced over her shoulder.

"Coffee?"

"Decaf please. High-octane raises me up and sets me
down. I'll do better on the road without it."

"Then look over that menu for solid food. Half and
half and sugar?"

"Just half and half."

Adrian brought his coffee. He kept his eyes on the
menu while she poured, but a quick glance at her left hand
revealed an empty ring finger. When she shuffled back a
step, he hoped she hadn't noticed. She drew a pad of tickets
and a pen from a pocket in the leaves and waited.

"Should I make myself scarce a while longer?"

"Not necessary." He looked up. "Can I order
breakfast?"

She pointed toward the top of the menu. "Anytime,
like it says."

"Yeah, there. How about a Number One? Fried and
over easy, the whites cooked, the yolks runny but hot, you
know, the impossible egg. Crisp bacon and home fries,
whole wheat toast. Could you go light on the butter and
only one tin of jam? And since this is a fifties place, how
about eight quarters for the juke and a small glass of
grapefruit juice?"

Adrian smiled, showing even, gleaming teeth. Grey
reached for his wallet. After she took his two dollars, he
returned to the distraction of the juke. With the chrome-
tipped handles that extended through the curved slot in the
bottom, he turned the stiff pages. Hank Locklin, real
country. He'd pass, as that was most of the day's radio fare
when he found music. Jerry Lee Lewis. Nope. He thought of
Lesley and decided he would call after dinner. Perry Como.

No way. She would ask how his mother was and how late would he get home. The Kingston Trio. Getting better. He didn't know when he'd get in and might need to find a motel. Early Beatles. We're getting somewhere. She would repeat the question about his mother. He would say that the old gal was better and glad he came. The new place would be good enough. The Eagles. All right. He probably would get a motel. Somehow he would see her shrug and would ask what she was thinking. Linda Ronstadt, a true lamenter. She would say it would be nice if he would push on and ask how much time he killed walking. Emmy Lou Harris, a sweeter wailer than Linda. He would say hardly any and wonder what difference getting home tonight would make. Rita Coolidge, "If You Could See Me Now." That's the place to start. He hummed a line: "If you could see me now, the one who said that he'd never roam."

"Pardon me." Adrian stood at the edge of his table. "You're going to need these," she said.

She held out her left hand, long tawny arm extended, long fingers curved into a little basket from which she spilled the coins into his. Buy the right music, he imagined her fingers saying. Play the right songs for your dream of me. He searched her face for details to remember in a motel room in Payune. Her mouth seemed to be working to hold something back. Perhaps she knew he would take her image with him, skin and shape and motion to be remembered.

Her face became serious. "Snow's coming," she said, her throaty voice informative, convincing. "This might be too much music."

When Adrian left, Grey trickled the coins, eight songs for a fantasy he would flesh out with the image of her, onto the table one-by-one. The coins stared up at him. In their graying surfaces he tried to see Lesley and was rewarded with the two of them in bed without embrace, with no more touch than a ritual peck goodnight before their heads hit distant pillows, his eyes searching the ceiling for the image of someone else. He turned back to the juke and slotted six of the coins, keeping two to fiddle with. Snow or not, Payune was close enough for a dozen songs.

HE TRIED TO REMEMBER when he began fantasizing an affair. No luck there, but it always came down to a single encounter with an interested stranger at a chance meeting on safe ground with no reruns and minimal risk. At first he told himself he would never have the chance, then that he would not take it, later that he probably wouldn't, then that he might not. The opportunity would be a test he would hope to pass by not seizing it. Then he could tell Lesley what he had not done, and they would begin renewal. Failure would mean a new, more dangerous habit than the fantasies that had been building on themselves like a drug in need of more of itself. That thought straightened him up. Arching his back against the seat, stretching his legs under the table, he rolled his neck in slow circles against the stiffness, trying to exorcise the devil he had hung there.

In front of him Adrian worked the grill. He closed his eyes. He had never come close to anything like an actual attractive stranger standing before him in her roadside place on a maybe snowy night. He chuckled. He was kidding himself. A little snow wouldn't be enough to keep him off the roads, and there were motels at least as close as Payune.

The smell of bacon brought him out of his trance. He wanted to stay in it, keep his eyes shut, imagine her saying something friendly, something warm, but he knew she was right there, waiting with his dinner.

"Pardon me," she said before he opened his eyes, in that tenor voice.

Grey rubbed his hands through his hair and looked up. Leaning forward, Adrian placed a heavy earthenware plate on the table and topped off his coffee. He breathed in the smell of bacon and eggs and the closeness of her body. She stood back.

"How far are you going?"

"Four hours east."

"Twice that tonight."

"I smelled snow, but the sky is mostly clear. Couldn't be soon, or much."

"Take a look."

Grey leaned toward the window and peered through the blinds. Big flakes swirled in the pale roadside neon. His car was covered with almost an inch of snow.

"Oh boy!" he said. Snow still made him feel like a kid, even when it posed a problem. Tonight it did, and he liked it even more.

"They're calling this a storm watch, not a warning," she said with a shrug. "They've got it wrong."

Grey wanted to quiz her, but she was moving down the aisle toward an old couple seating themselves in the booth at the end farthest from the big jukebox, the customary place, he decided, for an old pair who looked like part of the furniture. Turning to his food, he tried to listen to the pleasantries they shared with a familiar hostess. He twisted around and saw them sitting side-by-side, shoulders touching. Adrian leaned in front of them, reaching across to fill the farther cup with coffee, revealing the firm line of her breasts. When she straightened up, the old woman frowned at him, and Adrian glanced his way. He turned back to his meal to avoid her eyes.

Adrian's eggs were just right, the whites cooked through, the yolks hot and needing to be mopped up with the toast, her potatoes and bacon crisp, not too greasy and plenty of both, her toast buttered with restraint, her juice tart and cold. Grey was mopping yolk from the first egg when Adrian returned.

"How's the breakfast?" she asked.

"First-rate."

"Would you like more low-octane?"

Grey smiled and nodded. She poured and looked right at him.

"When it snows like this the motels in Payune fill up," she said.

"No time for all I put into that juke then."

"You're more than half an hour from Payune the way things are, and it's going to get worse."

"That's going to put me at the back of the line."

"You won't find another place until the interstate."

"That's two hours."

"Could be four tonight, maybe more. This storm is going there, too."

"What's your best advice?"

Adrian came a step closer to the booth, the coffee pot still aloft in one hand. She gazed through the blinds, her lips creased in contemplation. She canted her head to a thoughtful tilt. Grey's heart raced. He turned his eyes away and joined her in watching the furious snow.

"Get to Payune quick as you can. That's your best bet."

They watched together in awkward silence. When Grey glanced up, Adrian's eyes were waiting, holding, he thought, a sympathetic search for his understanding that he ought to be leaving as soon as possible.

"There must be cabins around here," he said.

"There's the Magruders ahead a few miles in the direction you're going, and the Davenports another ten, and the state park farther still. Probably filled with hunters and fishermen coming out of the woods. Big snows drive them out. You could call."

"Wished I'd looked for vacancy signs. The radio was on but I was hardly listening."

"The folks who were are grabbing them."

"How about a cup of the real stuff for the road?" he asked.

"You said it lifts you up and sets you down. That's not good for what you're facing."

Her interest felt good. "Thanks for your concern," he said. "I don't deserve it."

"Probably not." Again she looked out the window. "How about I call ahead? I know these folks. They might do me a favor. It's good business, you know. Or you could call motels in Payune. It's probably too late, though."

"If I hadn't made a fool of myself, I'd ask if I could just sleep in my car."

Adrian put the coffee pot on the table. "You'd freeze. You know that."

"Well, I'm not your problem."

"Seems like you are." She shook her head. "You sure have been looking at me. That makes it a bigger one."

He scratched at his forehead. "Bad habit. It's how pretty you are."

She sat down across from him. "It's not the first time a man tried to memorize me."

"I think you're amused."

"A little, but it's mostly a woman's relief from

deciding you're harmless. I don't worry about the ones who only memorize me. They're just taking me off to dreamland."

Grey looked down at his coffee cup and fiddled with it. "You're adding to my embarrassment," he said.

"That's your problem. What will you do with your memory of me?"

He shifted and started to look away.

"I'm sorry." She smiled and shook her head. "I never asked anyone that before. Don't know what got into me. It's as impolite as your staring."

He felt her concentration like a spotlight on an actor alone on a stage. He raised his eyes and looked right at her, hoping for words.

"I really shouldn't have," she said. "That's a man's business."

"Shouldn't you be thinking about those folks in the last booth?"

"Sitting here will keep them from grumping about you," she answered. "They'll think I know you."

"I don't want you to make me your problem."

"You already said that, so listen. I'm a fool to be thinking about my hide-a-bed. I'd have to move it in here from the storeroom. You'd have the customers' men's room. It's not much. But I don't know."

"I can't believe you're even thinking about that."

Adrian looked toward the kitchen, then down at her lap as though she were trying to gather something together inside. Two loose strands of copper hair framed her face when she brought it up, not to meet his eyes but to peer through the window. She stared into the snow, perhaps, he thought, to be sure of its magnitude, or to recheck her judgment of him, or of herself, but that was just more of kidding himself. She pulled her braid from behind her and fiddled with it until her eyes came back around to stay on his.

"My boy sleeps upstairs. On stormy nights the wind whistles right through his windows. He cries out and comes to my room. That's why you'd have to stay in here. Even so, I don't know."

"I don't remember when I got over being afraid of thunderstorms. Snow was different. It settled me. Even a storm."

"I wouldn't be comfortable having a stranger here."

She turned back toward the window. He fixed on her profile, long straight nose, prominent cheekbones, rusty freckles.

"He'll be coming in soon." The cleft in her chin added a fascinating masculine touch.

"Where is he?" Grey asked.

"Out in the snow." For a moment she had the far off glassy look of a dreamer, but when she turned and looked straight at him, he knew she was coming back to hard facts.

"I should call for him," she said. "It's time he came in."

As she scooted out of the booth and left for the front door, Grey fiddled with the quarters he hadn't slotted. He stared at the jukebox, the empty plate, the coffee pot Adrian had left on the table. He reached for the pot and topped off his cup, taking his time, drawing out every minute. The bells outside the door chimed softly. He could hear Adrian calling out for her boy, Davey, each call more distant than the one before.

It was time to go. He laid ten dollars on the table and rose, picking up the coffee pot to offer a refill to the old couple, laughing at this gesture he didn't understand. The old couple stood at the cash register, eyeing him.

"Adrian's out rounding up her boy." he said as he approached.

"We know," the woman said. "We're waiting." The man chewed a toothpick.

"I'll just get her," Grey said. He left quickly.

ON THE SNOW-COVERED STEPS, the wind blew flakes into his face, forcing him to squint and shield his eyes. He liked calling out Adrian's name and laughed at himself for thinking she would put him up. He remembered Lesley once saying that someday he would give himself to a woman who gave him attention. Adrian was giving him attention, in a manner of speaking, showing concern in spite of the way he had behaved. Calling out her name as he walked toward the road, leaning into the wind and snow, was his small return for what she had even thought about doing for him, making for a better exchange than he deserved. He would find her and remind her of the old couple, thank her, tell her not to worry and that he would creep south on the interstate to get below the storm where there might be a vacancy. That would be the end of it. At home he could remind Lesley of her prediction and tell her what he had not done.

No, he thought, this has not gone far enough to warrant that. Saying anything would cause more trouble than gain.

Then Adrian was there, a shadow peering east toward Payune. She turned and walked toward him through the swirling neon in small steps, huddling in on herself. She came close, using him as a shield against the snow. Looking right at him, she shook her head.

"I don't have a cup," she said.

"Geez, look what I've got. I was trying to help that old couple." He grinned and offered her the pot. "They weren't interested."

She looked at the door. "I forgot about them."

"I left money at the booth. I'll stay out here until Davey gets back."

"No need for that. He called from out back. I should have known he wouldn't stay by the road."

"Will you take this?" He held the pot out to her again. "I want to check the road."

"I just did." She took in a big breath. "It's time we went inside. There aren't going to be any vacancies in Payune."

"I'd like to stay out here a minute."

"Suit yourself," she said without taking the coffee pot. "I need to tell my boy your name."

"Why?"

"You've got to stay."

He looked toward the sign for Payune. Its letters were covered.

"I'm Grey. I'm still going to take a look."

"Suit yourself." She moved around him and started toward the diner. "There's a phone behind the counter," she shouted over her shoulder. "There's another in my kitchen if you need privacy while I'm closing down."

Grey went the other way, following Adrian's collapsed footsteps through more than three inches of snow. From the crest of the road he squinted eastward toward Payune, imagining himself hunched over the steering wheel in search of the lost right and centerlines, creeping along, fighting the wind, and, sooner rather than later, fatigue. He saw Lesley hovering over the road, and the "No Vacancy" signs in Payune, and the road beyond it cutting through the last hills for the farm country where the wind would blow the snow in hard, flat lines, then finally the lines of cars coming off the Interstate for the bigger motels where he might have a chance. He saw Lesley again, this time waiting for his call, listening to the radio for weather reports. If it was snowing at home, she would have called his mother by now.

Grey was tired, really tired. It was no trick on himself by the part of his mind that wanted to stay for the wrong reason, the impossible dream. In good weather, he could drive home tired, but Adrian was right about the time it would take tonight and that he probably couldn't make it. The look on her face, the look of one who was not comfortable with the way this was going but couldn't feel good about sending him on, was a road report he could rely on.

FROM THE MIDDLE OF THE BROAD AISLE, Grey looked toward the inner door that led to Adrian and Davey's home, hoping to see the boy who might lighten this awkward time. He glanced at the money Adrian hadn't picked up and at the juke still playing his mournful songs. Only then did he stop to look at her behind the counter, scraping the grill, and contemplate the prospect of being her unwanted guest. She twisted around and looked at him.

"Looking for a job?"

"Sure."

"For starters, just give me that coffee pot you've been wearing. I might let you off the hook, being as tired as you are."

He took it to her. "I tried to give it to you outside."

"I was preoccupied. What's your last name?"

"Hart."

She turned away from the grill to face him. "Mr. Hart, I don't know what to do with you."

"I don't know what to do with me either. Maybe Davey will keep me busy."

"That's likely the price you'll pay for being here. You don't have kids, do you?"

"Right. Maybe it won't feel like a price."

She turned, folded her arms, leaned her hips against the grill. "That would be nice for him," she whispered.

"Here's the coffee pot."

"Don't you need to call home?"

"That's really on your mind."

"Aren't you going to call the person you're wearing that ring for?"

"I just got this undeserved and unexpected invitation. I wanted to say thanks first. And find my sea legs."

"Please do. Davey will be wanting your attention as soon as he's in his PJs. He has been asking, and he'll have lots of questions."

"Which phone?"

"It's your call, Mr. Hart. I can only keep him away for a while."

The coffee pot lightened in his hand and seemed to rise on its own. He looked down to see Adrian's hand cradling it, then up at her strong face with its persistent hint of what he took to be amusement.

His stomach twinged. "Thanks a lot for this," he said, giving up the coffee pot and leaving to make his call.

HE MADE IT in Adrian's kitchen near a double window pelted by wind-driven snow. Davey watched and listened from the door, running back and forth to his mother, calling out information and questions as he ran. Who is he calling, Mama? Does he have a wife? Is he going to stay? They are talking about the snow stopping him. Where will he sleep? Grey could not quite hear Adrian's answers but felt her soft, firm admonitions for Davey to lower his voice, making it difficult to concentrate on Lesley.

The snow there was hard enough to make her worry. She asked where he was. He told her about the diner fourteen miles on the far side of Payune without mentioning its name. When he paused, she filled the silence with the obvious question about when he would be home. He was too tired to push on. She asked where he would stay.

He told her how bad the snow was, about the hunter's cabins and all the no vacancy signs. He went on too long.

"You can go another fourteen miles."

"The motels in Payune are probably full."

"How do you know that?"

Grey swallowed. "The woman who runs this place told me."

"What did she tell you to do?"

"Les, the snow is probably too bad to do anything, and I'm beat."

"But what did she tell you to do?"

"We talked about calling ahead, but she said it would be of no use. She's a local. She went out to the road and came back really discouraged. This isn't making her happy."

Lesley cleared her throat. He knew he had not pulled off matter-of-fact well enough to reassure her.

"You said 'we'." It must have been quite a conversation."

"She was trying to help me solve a problem."

"And so, you're...?"

"She's going to let me stay here. She's not happy about it, but she has a little boy that...."

"That's all she's got?"

"Yes."

"A single woman. What difference does the boy make?"

"Something for me to do, I hope. He seems interested. Adrian, that's her name, says he'll want my attention."

Davey skittered away from the door calling out to his mother that the man was going to give him attention. He returned bearing a big grin.

"So, you're calling her by her first name already?"

"Look, I don't know her last name. She's wearing a nametag. Look, I'm here for the night. On a hide-a-bed in the middle of a restaurant. I'll be sleeping between a row of booths and a counter with swivel chairs. Very cozy. What else can I do?"

She wanted him to push on, take it easy, drive through the night, get south on the interstate as quickly as possible to maybe get out of the worst of it. He explained how he had fallen asleep waiting for his dinner and started to repeat what Adrian had said about how bad things were, but Lesley cut him off.

"You're so naive you don't know when a woman is trying to keep you there. A woman is interested and you can't see that you're lapping it up."

"Les, this is hard for her. What's it like there?"

"Is she interesting?"

Grey described her as plain talking, matter-of-fact. He felt like an imposition and hoped her boy wouldn't keep him up too late.

"A boy without a father," she said. "A door to a woman's heart."

"Okay, I'll leave."

The boy ran from the door and yelled to his mother that Grey was leaving.

"Grey, I...never mind. It doesn't really matter, does it?" Then another pause. "Can you get an early start?"

"I hope so. Driving in daylight should help even if it's still snowing." He paused. "There is going to be a lot of snow."

"They expect it to stay bad through tomorrow. I hate to think of you stuck there with a young woman for so long, if she's attractive."

"Lesley, stop worrying."

"Is she?"

"Sort of."

"Are you thinking about her?"

He tried to conceal a deep breath. "Nothing is going to happen, Lesley. I don't do that sort of thing."

"But will you tell me if it does?"

"It won't."

"But would you?"

"I'll tell you all about the nothing that happens."

"And nothing about what does."

"Good night, Lesley." He knew they would not find an agreeable place to stop. He hung up the phone.

LOOKING INTO THE DARKNESS outside Adrian's kitchen window, Grey pictured Lesley sitting at their kitchen table, staring at the phone, twirling a glass of wine. Protected by telephone distance, he had used mostly honest words that still planted fear. He wondered if he wanted that. Would it shake things up or take things down? Which did he want? He waited for Adrian's image to replace hers but could not rid his mind of that dark picture of his wife with her hand on the glass and the sadness in her eyes, the sadness he hid in his imaginings. She might sip that wine all night, to numb the taste of her man in another woman's kitchen waiting for something to happen.

A milky floodlight outside the kitchen window burst on and flesh-toned the swirl of a million blowing snowflakes. The boy stood close to Grey, looking out at the storm that brought them together, his little fingers lingering on a light switch between the window and the back door. He stared up at Grey through eyes held wide and round under dark, up-curving lashes. His thumb, covered by a corner of a discarded tee shirt, was in his mouth. Grey knew it was time to give the boy his attention, and as a welcome side effect, fill his own awkward time.

"It's snowing," the boy said through the muffle of the tee shirt.

"Sure is. I bet I know your name, young fella." The words came with surprising ease.

"My mama told you!" he replied.

"Did you know I was sleeping over tonight?"

The boy's face lit up. "I heard you tell somebody that on the phone. Then my mama told me. Was that your wife?"

"Sure was."

"Uh huh. Do you have a boy?"

"Nope. No boy, no girl. Just me and my wife."

Davey turned and stepped close enough to the window to push his nose against a lower pane. When Grey did the same three panes higher, he looked up and grinned from ear to ear.

"My mama says don't stick your tongue on the glass in the winter or you'll be in a world of hurt. Noses are okay."

"Thanks for the warning, big fella."

"I'm not a big fella. I'm a boy."

"Who can be a darn good waiter."

"You're right about that!"

"So, what are we going to do tonight? This is your home, so you get to call the shots."

"I get to what?"

"Call the shots. Decide what we're going to do."

"We're going outside!" Davey yelled.

"No way!" Adrian stood in the door behind them, leaning against the frame, arms crossed, almost smiling. "Maybe in the morning. Why don't you guys play a game?"

"Checkers," Davey yelled. He ran right past her.

"He'll wear you out if you let him," Adrian said.

"I'll let him."

Adrian sagged against the doorframe. She started to speak but stopped and looked toward the window. Grey figured that the boy's needs were tender ground. Turning away, she left before Grey could say that this was the least he could do.

FOR NEARLY TWO HOURS, Davey pursued competence in a game he must have only begun to learn. Grey's occasional advice passed through a ritual of squinting eyes and creasing brows lasting half a minute before the boy decided upon a hint or suggested move. Davey was as earnest as he had been as a waiter, but checkers needed vigilance and endurance, and he showed that, too.

Adrian had been passing by the table on her way to one errand after another. Then she was in a purple terrycloth bathrobe and slippers over thick socks, the picture of staying warm on a cold, snowy night. He was surprised until he looked at the clock over the door to her living room. The night was pushing eight o'clock.

"He doesn't see all the possibilities yet," she said on the fourth or fifth trip. "Double and triple jumps, stuff like that."

Davey stiffened, and Grey stiffened with him. With each maternal remark the boy frowned and opened his eyes wide in search of Grey's support. Grey nodded, hoping Adrian would see his complicity. He wished Davey would say something.

Adrian's trips into the kitchen continued, but the comments stopped. Once, when she was watching, Grey had a triple jump all the way to Davey's end for a quick king that would have tipped the balance of power beyond recovery. He stopped at double and looked up. Adrian smiled. On her next trip she parked herself behind Davey's chair and leaned over him, pulling the top of her robe up against her neck. Her hair draped her shoulders.

"There's a double jump on the upper left," she whispered. "You can get kinged."

Davey made a triangle of his arms and propped his chin on his hands. He started to look at Grey but dropped his eyes to the board as though he had decided not to look for support. Adrian stayed put.

"Are you playing?" Davey asked.

"Sure am. It's your move."

"Guess I forgot," the boy said.

Grey flashed on a memory of one of his own early stands against a zealous father who wanted the learning to come before its time. It was a game of gin with his favorite uncle, his elbows stretching to reach the surface of the table, his little hands gripping the cards, his father behind him, advising each move, Uncle Ted glowering his disapproval. Grey mocked a frown at Adrian and nodded her toward the door. Almost against her will, her face broke into a grin. She straightened up and chuckled. With mock prim, she adjusted herself like a chastened schoolgirl.

"I'm going to take a bath," she said, turning for the door. "I'll make hot chocolate later."

Grey resisted watching her go. When Davey looked up, he was waiting for him.

"I don't want you to have kings," the boy announced,

his hand poised on a checker, "so I'm gonna do this instead of the double jump." It was more of a question.

"Good idea."

He jumped Grey's checker closest to his own back line and relaxed, the move made, the mother gone.

"Your move," Davey muffled through his tee shirt, free hand bobbing its other end, little face determined, big eyes more tired than needy.

ADRIAN RETURNED ONLY TWICE. First, while her bath water roiled beyond the wall, she brought them fresh-squeezed grapefruit juice. After the bath she arrived in blue jeans and a heavy, loose-fitting sweater to serve hot chocolate. She kept to herself, wandering about the room, tidying up, glancing through the blinds, only a few times passing close to the table. Grey surprised himself by hardly noticing her, so absorbed had he become in the life of a child who drew energy from him without end. Though he was tiring, he decided to wait for Davey to have enough.

He looked up to see Adrian leaning on the doorframe. Not wanting mother and son to see him distracted, Grey doubled his effort to concentrate on the game, but she was there on the side of his vision, brushing her hair with one hand and pulling at tangles with the other. Wet, it hung straight as a curtain to the small of her back. She seemed to be soaking in this strange domestic scene with a wistful look. Grey wondered how bittersweet this must taste to her, how like a contentment she must often imagine. The moment had fullness worthy of remembering for its own sake, no matter what else came, but his fantasy rose with the thought and would not diminish.

He moved a checker forward from his back line, then looked up. Adrian was gone.

"You missed a double-jump," Davey said with sagging enthusiasm, his hand moving in slow motion toward one of his checkers. With no fanfare, he executed a killing triple jump of Grey's kings, landing on the far end of Grey's side of the board.

"King me," he said, his voice creeping out. "I'm gonna

beat you this time."

Though cornered and nearly vanquished, Grey played out a defense, mostly a retreat from overwhelming numbers. He stretched it out for Davey to savor the chase and the victory. After nearly five minutes, he knew the boy would accept surrender.

"You're the winner, little buddy. Want to quit?"

Davey nodded. He took the tee shirt from his lap, put it in his mouth, and began to suck so hard his Adam's apple moved like a piston.

"Are you ready for bed?"

The boy shrugged.

"How about a ride? I'll take you to your mother."

"You take me upstairs and read to me."

"Shouldn't we ask?"

"I'll tell her."

ADRIAN SAT CROSS-LEGGED in an overstuffed chair in front of one of the windows that flanked the front door. A wall lamp cast a soft glow over her as she brushed her hair. With each stroke it thickened into a cascade of copper waves. She smiled at what she saw, Grey carrying her boy into the living room. Davey twisted away from Grey and extended his arms toward his mother.

"Grey's gonna read to me, Mama."

Adrian rose, crossed the room, and came over to her boy's outstretched arms.

"You won't miss much," Davey said, pulling her to him, keeping Grey so close he could smell Adrian's shampoo and the freshness of her skin.

"Goodnight, Davey," she said, kissing him and patting his cheeks, then pulling out of his embrace. The boy let go and snuggled against Grey's chest. The mother's restrained smile glowed like a low fire on the other side of a screen. She tousled Davey's hair.

"Go on now," she whispered. "It's time."

Davey was asleep before they reached the top of the stairs. The wind howled, and branches scratched his bedroom window. The shades were drawn shut, the blankets pulled back. A tired, balding teddy, a gift from another generation, lay on the side of his pillow, waiting. Grey put Davey down like he would place a delicate gift just after taking it out of the box. He covered him up and wondered whether the child neither he nor Lesley thought they wanted would have made a difference. The boy opened his eyes to slits and reached for his teddy, pulling it close. No tee shirt in his mouth, no fingers bobbing, just the teddy tucked under his chin, and a filled-up look on his face. Grey watched him for a few moments, shut off the lamp next to the bed, and left the room.

He paused on the landing to look at pictures on the wall, hoping to find a father. None was there.

SHE HAD ANGLED the over-stuffed chair toward the window and drawn up the blinds. An outdoor light brightened snow falling even thicker than when Grey and Davey watched through the kitchen window a few hours before. She had opened the couch bed and made it with a beige bottom sheet, a top one of autumn leaves, a light brown wool blanket, two dark brown fluffy pillows, and a dark green quilt. The bottom of the bed almost reached her chair. Hands clasped behind her head, legs tucked under, she watched the snow. Grey stood at the bottom of the stairs, hands in his pockets, unsure where to sit or what to do.

"You didn't miss any story," he said. "He fell asleep on the stairs."

She twisted around to face him, scrunching up her knees to fit in the chair sideways, circling her arms around her legs.

"Thanks for filling him up," she said.

Grey nodded and looked around. "I liked it. I had a good time."

"He's going to make a big deal of you in the morning. He'll be your alarm clock."

"I'll need an early start."

"In this?" She pointed at the window. "There's going to be a lot of it. You'll have to wait for the crews to clear the road. It's possible they won't get it done until very late."

"Do you mind my asking something about him?"

"You want to know about his father. He soaked you up like a dry sponge, and you're wondering."

"Will this make him think about him?"

"There's no father to think about. The man has never come to see him. Never. Davey can only think about the idea of a father."

"I'm sorry. Maybe I shouldn't have asked."

"If you hadn't been willing to pretend, I wouldn't have answered. I might have said it was none of your business." She sighed. "You fleshed it out for him."

"Maybe I overdid it."

"You were great." She laughed. "You even put me in my place."

Grey took in extra air. "It started out as my escape. I didn't know what to do here. He became my buddy, and I took his side against you."

She grinned big and shook her head. "The right side."

"Thanks for letting me shoo you out the door."

Adrian raised her legs and pressed her knees into her chest. Grey felt the probe of her eyes.

"You don't talk with your wife, do you?"

Grey sat on the arm of the couch, diagonally across from her, the farthest possible distance.

"I've forgotten how."

"Just tell her what's in your head."

"What do you think is in my head?"

"You tell me."

He looked away, then back, right at her. "Right now, you."

"That's it." Her voice was soft and low. "Tell her it's come to that. Soon."

"It's lust," Grey said, surprising himself with his directness. "That's how it started this evening, and that's what it still is, mostly."

"You brought it here with you. And that's still all it is."

"There's a bit of something else now."

"Not enough to matter. You know that."

"I don't know what to do."

"Neither do I."

Their eyes locked, and Grey's heart beat in his ears.

"Talk to her," Adrian said.

"Whom do you talk to?"

"Nobody in the way you mean. Nobody I'm responsible to like you are. But if I was in your situation, I would have started talking long before I have something to rescue. I've heard it works sometimes."

Grey looked away.

"Come look at this snow and tell me about your early start."

He walked around the bed and stood a few feet behind her chair. For a minute or so they watched the snow batter against the window. It seemed to pound in harmony with the heartbeat pulsing from his chest to his head. He couldn't remember hearing the wind pounding like that in the kitchen or in Davey's room, or his heart like that in a long time. He wondered how long this snow would keep him here and knew the same question preoccupied Adrian.

She stood up and faced him. "You're going to feel crazier and crazier till you start talking with your wife."

"Generally, I hide everything in..." He shook his head. "Never mind."

"Fantasies?"

"You could say so." He paused again. "And now I can't get lust out of the way."

"That's a tall order, big as you've let it grow."

"Has that ever happened to you?"

"Only when it grew where it shouldn't."

"Has it?"

"It gave me Davey. But you're asking about now. No, but you got inside my head when you set me aside for my boy." She took in a deep, slow breath. "I don't want to light the fuse."

"Mine or yours?"

"Yours is lit already." She turned toward her bedroom door. "I'm going to bed now."

"To sleep on it?"

"We've both got plenty to sleep on. Others to think about."

"I wish I could keep that in mind all the time."

"It takes work. And doesn't always work."

His heart pumped another extra beat. "I thought you wanted me to sleep in the diner."

"That's a cold dreary place to put a guest."

With folded arms she walked past him. At her bedroom door, she turned and stood framed in lamplight from behind. Her arm reached out to the wall inside her door.

"You want something too, don't you?" he asked.

"It might be nice, but it's not enough."

"The first part of that is nice to know, anyway."

"Well, it's the thought that counts. Right?"

"Yes, right."

"Good night, Grey." She switched off the light, then shut the door most of the way. He decided that the narrow space left open was for listening for her boy, should the storm awaken him. The snow blew hard enough against the windows to awaken a boy as tired as Davey, if he was like Adrian said he was.

GREY WENT TO THE FRONT DOOR and switched off the outside light. He sat on the edge of the bed and listened for the sounds of Adrian undressing, hearing some, imagining what he wished to see. Sweater stretching over skin, hook unhooking, breasts revealed, nipples chilled erect. Zipper pulling down, legs stepping out of jeans, panties slipping over buttocks, the pile of clothes beneath her until she moved toward her bed. Cover sliding back, rustling of sheets, a deep breath, a sigh. He lay back on the pillow and closed his eyes. Davey was there, staring across the checkerboard, feeding on the game, on him, hungry like himself. He tried to imagine sitting with Lesley in their kitchen, talking about this night, but pictures of Adrian intruded. He rose and began to undress, not so much for sleep but to move. Down to underwear, he lay down again and pulled the covers over him, cold sheets on electric skin.

He closed his eyes and let the day reel through his mind: Adrian sitting across from him in his booth, tossing back a strand of hair; the moving landscape of the road; fur-hooded Davey scraping boots on the floor; Adrian behind the counter taking the coffee pot from his hand with that smile he thought might have been tinged with amusement; her hazy form coming toward him from the road; the shape of her breasts and buttocks pushing through the flowers of her dress; Davey's hand sliding checkers across the board, his big tired eyes looking at him from across the table; clothes dropping to the floor; the boy's head on the pillow; her copper mane and freckled skin. The pictures sped by, lost shape, broke into a kaleidoscope of color and form, reformed, broke up, faded.

The wind scratched branches against the window. Grey began a relaxation exercise Lesley had taught him in the good early days, the best days, before they were married. Starting with his feet, he relaxed each muscle from his toes to the crown of his head and back down, taking time for each until gravity pulled his body down to dead weight and some bodiless, mysterious part of him rose through the flotsam of pictures to a not quite empty place where whatever returned might more easily be discarded.

The room brightened in surprising flickers of moonlight. From the bedroom came faint sounds, the creak of a bed, feet hitting the floor and padding across it, intrusions that transformed into a luminous, naked Adrian. She walked to her door and stood there in an open robe, staring into the living room, then at the stairs, listening. She drew her robe around her and leaned against the doorframe for only a moment before she withdrew into her room, leaving the door wide open.

The flotsam returned. Pieces of Highway 47 sped by. Darkened houses, crummy junkyards, closed gas stations, Lesley hovering over the car, opaque, fading. A blue neon dot in the trees becoming Adrian's Diner, becoming Adrian at the grill, sitting across from him in his booth, moving toward him in the snow, hovering over her boy at the kitchen table, standing by the door in her opened robe. Now, smiling with closed lips, she walked to within a step of his bed. She took the last step forward. Her hands went to her shoulders and pushed the robe off. It dropped to the floor.

She hovered there. Grey tried to hold her there, drink her in, but she dissolved. With deep, slow breaths he tried to bring her back. He wanted her back like a boy's first thrilling dream. She re-formed, but gusts of wind blew her away, and branches scratching hard again on the windows distracted him like nails dragged across a chalkboard. The gusts and scratches faded and returned over and over, each quieter and more distant than the one before until they became a soothing rhythm punctuated by pelts of snow and flickers of moonlight. He waited for sleep.

Sheets shifted on themselves, silky sounds, then a long, soft sigh. They were standing at a window on a sunny winter morning in a bright kitchen that smelled of coffee, bacon and hot cinnamon biscuits. Outside, Davey pushed through snow that rose almost to his armpits. His breath blew steam, and the snow muffled his call for Grey to come outside. The snow became sand on a sunny beach where the boy built castles and called for him to join in, then turned back into the darkened room where Grey lay alone. A little voice cried out from far away, calling for someone, but the wind smothered it. Adrian came toward him, robe on again and open, flesh showing in a long strip down the center of her, hair spilling over her shoulders. Her hands went to them, and the robe fell. With a shake of her head, she threw her hair behind her, mounted the bed on hands and knees, and inched forward, sliding her knees along Grey's legs, pushing in on his thighs. She began to lower herself over him and reached for the edge of the quilt. So close. He drank her in and raised his hands to hold her sides and pull her to him. The wind surged, and behind it the far-off cry returned, growing louder. Adrian straightened and cocked her head. She dropped the covers from her hand and retreated. Grey's thighs came un-trapped, the pressure gone. He pushed himself up.

Adrian stood at her doorway, pushing an arm through a sleeve of her robe, looking toward the stairway. The crying softened and came closer, and little footsteps padded on the stairs. She turned toward Grey, her robe hanging from a single shoulder. In what seemed like slow motion, she stretched her uncovered arm behind her until she found the other sleeve, not for a second taking her eyes away from Grey, gathering her robe around her.

"It's Davey," she said. "Pull up those covers, Grey." She tied off her robe. "Go back to sleep."

He lay back on the pillow.

Davey paused at the foot of the stairs, tee shirt dangling from his mouth, secure in his harbor before he docked. Grey strained to watch as he shuffled across the living room, buried his head in the folds of his mother's robe, wrapped his arms around her legs. She held him there.

"You're so warm, Mama," he muttered.

"Come to bed with me, love." She started to turn, but Davey held her there and looked toward Grey.

"Grey's awake, Mama." He looked up at her. "Maybe I could ask him if I could sleep in his bed."

The boy ran to the side of Grey's bed and bounced on his bottom before Adrian could stop him.

"He won't mind," Davey mumbled through his mouthful of thumb and shirt.

Adrian, shaking her head, came to the bed and sat down next to him. With a slow, deep breath, she composed herself as she had done outside in the snow when she decided to let Grey stay. He wished to find steadiness like that to calm his unblanched need and his wonder at what might just have been aborted or he had only imagined.

"Davey, Grey's not going to stay here."

The boy looked back and forth between them, his long, up-curving eyelashes and darting eyes working overtime.

"I know," he said.

"This is not a good idea."

"It's just pretending."

"The snow is going to stop tomorrow, maybe sooner. He should be able to start for home."

"Tomorrow?"

"That's the weather forecast."

"Maybe there'll still be too much snow."

"You might be right, but it will be daytime, and the road crews might have cleared away a lot of snow."

"She's right, Davey," Grey said. "If I can, I will leave tomorrow. In the morning even. So I can get home before dark. It will be slow going."

Davey shrugged his little shoulders and bobbed his free hand up and down in the tee shirt.

"To your wife?"

"Right, Davey."

"It's just for tonight," he said.

Grey looked at Adrian for a signal, expecting a sign of disapproval, gentle but certain. Instead he got laughing eyes and a shake of disbelief.

"Davey, you need to ask him."

"I'd like it just fine," Grey said, returning his gaze.

Davey jumped up and darted for his mother's room.

"Are you sure about this?" Adrian asked.

"Are you?"

"I am. He wants to know what it's like."

"I'm not sure I'll know what to do."

"He'll drive. Just go along for the ride."

It would be a different ride than the one he wanted and knew he would have taken. He wanted to ask her questions, but Davey raced in. He thought she would not have answered anyway, at least not then. Only her boy mattered now. In the morning it would be no different. It was all about her boy now.

Davey had a pillow under each arm. His tee shirt, pinched in his teeth, dropped to the floor as he spoke. "You pretend too, Mama?" What began as a declaration became a question before it was finished, full of hope and doubt. Standing there with his load, eyes wide open, he waited for an answer.

"Sure, love," she said. "I'll be right back."

Davey arranged the pillows against the back of the bed. He climbed on and crawled toward Grey, then retreated to retrieve his tee shirt. When he settled in and looked up at Grey through his thumb-filled mouth, Grey patted the top of his head.

"Not goodnight till Mama's here."

Adrian came out of her bedroom. She stood in a trace of moonlight at the foot of the bed and gazed down on them, taking her time opening her robe. Her hands went to her shoulders and pushed it off. Boyish plaid pajamas covered her.

"Grey's Papa," Davey said.

"Just for tonight, Davey."

"Get in, Mama. Kiss us goodnight."

Adrian got in next to her son and settled on her side,

perching on her elbow. Grey rolled to his side, and the boy was surrounded.

"Say goodnight first," Davey said.

"Goodnight Davey," Grey said. "See you in the morning."

The boy ran his tee shirt along the fuzz of Grey's forearm. "Thanks," he said.

"Thank you."

"For what?"

"For wanting me to be here."

Grey bent down, kissed him on the forehead, then leaned out of the way. Adrian bent over her boy and kissed him on the cheek. "Goodnight, love," she said.

"Ga night, Mama," he mumbled in the softest voice. "Ga night, Grey." He looked back and forth between them with grapefruit eyes, sucking away on his tee shirt-covered thumb.

They were face-to-face over Davey. They started for each other without hesitation, their lips coming together with surprising fullness and softness, lingering for a moment, moistening, tasting each other over the watching boy. Adrian withdrew but remained so close Grey could feel her breath on his skin. Then she pulled back a little more.

"Goodnight," she said. "Sleep well."

"You, too," Grey said.

They stayed propped on their elbows and watched Davey. He reached out a few times to pat their heads through his tee shirt, his eyes narrowing as he faded into sleep. When Adrian lowered herself to her side, Grey did, too. In the flickers of moonlight he watched them both, the mother more.

It didn't take long for Davey to fall asleep. Over his easy breathing they looked at each other with innocent, embarrassed smiles, almost starting to laugh. Grey reached across and touched Adrian's cheek. She closed her eyes and took in a deep breath that raised her chest. With his forefinger he traced the line of her jaw, across her chin, around her lips and eyes, across her forehead, down the length of her nose.

"This has been good for me," Grey whispered. He noticed the thin lines of moonlight on her face, shaped like the blinds.

"It's been good for Davey, too." She started to turn to her back, but Davey stirred and rolled toward her. She planted a kiss on the tip of his nose, then pulled him in to her.

"Go to sleep now, love."

The boy didn't answer. Grey turned onto his back and stared at the ceiling.

"Has this been good for you?" he asked.

"I like it just fine."

She closed her eyes.

THE WIND HAD DROPPED to a suggestion, and the branches brushed the windows in a woody whisper. Through shuttered eyes Grey could feel the room brighten and dim as the moonlight came and went. The storm seemed to be ending sooner than expected. He turned to his side, away from Davey and Adrian. He would call Lesley and leave in the morning if the road crews would let him. Bone-tired at last, he felt himself sliding into a snowy ride on Highway 47's curving ups and downs. Lesley's wind chimes, crystal clear in a light breeze, drew him into their kitchen. He was trying to decide how much to tell her of what had and had not happened. He heard himself saying that it might not be worth the price, but he wasn't sure if the last half hour was or was not a dream. Lesley was asking all the hard questions and telling him that if there were no boy and Adrian had given him more, he would have taken it. She was right.

Lesley's face filled the glinty white tree canyon until Adrian, hovering over him naked, took her place and brought him back into wonder. Grey struggled not to go there, but he failed. In the morning, if he so much as mentioned the night, she would put a finger to her lips. If he asked about staying until the sun had loosened the snowpack, she would tell him how cold it was going to remain and remind him of who was waiting. She would make him a country breakfast in her own kitchen with good coffee and perfect eggs. Davey would be up early to play with him in the snow until breakfast, and she would say that's enough, he needs to get back to the way things are. They would sit at the table together until it was time to go. It would be a gift all around. He would try to value that more than what he had missed and not deserved.

Grey wondered how they would say goodbye. Davey would need to be there.

Highway 47 drew him from left to right, right to left, and back again, but always forward. He looked from side to side for draws leading to ridge tops and distant summits and imagined the open land beyond, all under a thick mantle of untrodden snow and a bright, clear, windless sky. Then Adrian appeared at her door, robe open, inviting, turning toward the stairs, drawing her robe around her, closing the curtain too soon. Or was it some hidden wisdom emerging to save him from his fantasy? Her image jarred him awake. He tried to think back from that sweet, uncertain moment, hoping to find what was real and what was not, but he stopped. There would be plenty of time in the car to think through that. Too much time over that slow road.

Davey shifted and settled on his back. The boy slept well now, and his mother, too.

Outside the air stood still, and the moonlight held. Grey let himself drift back to the road, gliding above the bumpy road ice, floating along in the cozy chamber of his car, his cell-like link from here to there. Up and down and around the snowy hills, through white-gilded trees toward Payune and the opening to the farm county, where the road began a straight shot toward the home and the wife he needed and struggled to see. The wind picked up enough to worry him, but the moonlight remained true. He hoped the storm was over. Wind chimes tinkled on a snowy deck, or bells by a restaurant door. A voice called out. He didn't know whose it was or what it said. He decided not to listen. He just drove on.

MOSCHOVITZ AND PASTERNAK

A MAN WITH A RUDDY FACE as tanned as soft leather and hair as white as snow stands sideways half a dozen people in front of me in line at a polling place in Chapel Hill. He waits and watches with a patience and curiosity no other early morning voter matches. With bright, clear eyes that seem filled with the satisfaction of well-spent years, he scans the room with obvious interest, as if he could not be more pleased to be here. Watching him, I am certain his eyes are offering an invitation to talk. But the crowd is impatient and inward, as if remaining aloof would hurry the procession through lines, registration tables, and voting booths to cars and freeways. Like the others, I came here enclosed in a cocoon, incubating myself for the daily rebirth of my life at work. I want to complete this task and be on my way, but watching someone who seems so pleased to be here changes me. I wonder if age alone explains him and if I will become as patient and observant, as content to stand in a long line. I wish I could move closer to him.

His eyes push out a bit too far from their sockets in a way I notice in some fellow Jews. *In a way,* I say to myself, because that caveat makes me more comfortable with my stereotype. I'm a Jew, I say to myself, I am entitled to recognize another Jew by his features. But I laugh at myself for this excuse that works for only one stereotype. I have others.

But more is going on inside me than absorbing this older man's warm, welcoming face. Surely I am taking in his Jewishness as much as his appeal. I feel a connection so strong it unsettles me, and I know why. I have always been ambivalent about membership identities that connect me with some and separate me from others. But here in the American Legion Hall, in a crowd of strangers, I assure myself no harm can come. I give myself a generous allowance for sentimentality and imagination.

The man's eyes contain a smile, a greeting I believe he cannot escape offering. *Shalom*, they say. To anyone. They wait for connection, but in its absence are as content with watching.

There are two lines crawling forward through the doors of the building, replicating the clogged highways everyone hopes to be riding soon. "A through L" seems bottlenecked and slow to divide for the two registration stations reserved for it at the tables. By comparison, "M through Z" breezes by. In their postures, faces and words, the occupants of the slow lane suggest envy and disbelief.

"Same mistake every year," says one. "You'd think they'd learn."

"Splitting the population right down the middle of the alphabet clearly doesn't work in this precinct," says another. She shakes her head.

A few more remarks, some half-smiles and light laughter, a few nodding heads. The stress of these folks seems to lessen, and they become more sociable. The old Jew turns in a full circle, trying, I think, to seize the opportunity for conversation.

Some Jews favor a separating identity. We are Members of the Tribe, it goes. I have felt little of this over the years, I haven't approved. In my judgment calling ourselves "The Tribe" creates unbridgeable distance from others, encourages us to grant ourselves a higher status no one deserves. I forget the centuries of persecution that can force any group to close in on itself behind circled wagons, that one way it does this is to regard itself as chosen. Many besides Jews have called themselves "The Chosen." Yet I pick from the crowd *another Jew*, though everyone in the room and waiting outside the door all the way to the parking lot is here in response to a social obligation that should be sufficient to bind us together without reference to culture or religion. For a moment my connection with these strangers pales next to the bond I feel with one person who looks so familiar to me because of his features. A man with whom I will probably never speak. Is he a stranger, or are we seeds from a single tree with roots in the ancient past, surviving in small, scattered groves all over the world? We are, but this should not be emphasized, I think. So many others can say this. So I mimic the old Jew. I look around a place intended to cross the separation and distance that cultural and ethnic, religious and national identity bring, the centuries of hate, warfare and persecution that are their bastard children. I decide to believe that this polling place puts my ancient identity to shame.

But I like staring at this handsome old man, and I am enjoying that he is a Jew. I don't want a self-inquisition denying me this sudden feeling of belonging that I don't get from the places where I think I should, such as this polling place. I don't want my disapproval to soil this unexpected, deep sense of connection, for it rises inside me like a spring welling up from some deep unreachable source at the base of a wooded bluff. Though I may never know this source, I want to feel the welling up. At least for a moment I want to know what this man must know.

I ask myself how I can read so much into eyes? Or a nose. His crags downward like an eagle's, pointing first to a small mouth that moves about with, I now decide, the slightest touch of impatience, but more for lack of contact than hurry, because our line is moving well. Below that mouth is a cleft in his square chin, a real Kirk Douglas dimple, a mark I associate with active men. He scrapes his lower teeth against his upper lip, then purses his lips together, the tip of his tongue occasionally protruding, moving from side to side. Is that another touch of impatience, I wonder, not for progress but for conversation? In that knit short sleeve shirt, those khaki shorts, that windbreaker tossed over his shoulder, he is not hurrying to work. He is headed for tennis or racquetball, the spa or the golf course. He is finished with the daily routine of freeways and finances. I envy him.

His body supports the inference that he is no aging couch potato. Small but athletically built and postured, straight-backed, trim in the belly, he stands at ease with legs apart, one hand clasping the other wrist behind his back. He rocks back and forth from heel to toe like a referee on a basketball court waiting for the end of a timeout. Now he folds his arms in front and trades his rocking for twisting at his waist to the ends of his range of motion. His broad shoulders have no forward bend, his arms still have visible muscle. He has been doing something healthy most every day, swinging a racket or a golf club, using his trim legs to carry him as often as a car does. I want to look like that in twenty years.

This is how I want him to be, I say inside. I am giving him an identity and wishing it for myself. Yet what I see I believe is true.

He is chatting now with a few complainers from "A through L" and doesn't notice "M through Z" splitting as it approaches the volunteers who will verify our registration. In two steps I am next to him, behind him. He returns to rocking forward and back. I see him *davening* in an Orthodox synagogue or at the Wailing Wall in Jerusalem, where I have never been. He completes another turn. He sees me.

Recognition. A silent *shalom*. He is as certain of me as I am of him.

"Are you a native of North Carolina?" he asks.

"No," I say. "Missouri by birth, then Colorado, California, now here." My standard short-form answer.

"New York, then Cleveland, then here," he says with a faint nasal edge, a remnant under flat Midwestern. "A Diaspora, so to speak. You know what I mean."

"I can hear the New York, just a bit."

He smiles. "I don't mind it's still here. What brings you here?"

The line is too short for more than a footnote. I give him highlights of my zigzag route to Chapel Hill through regions and careers. He smiles in recognition.

"Like my son. You'd tell me more if we had time."

An invitation, I think. "What brings you to Chapel Hill?"

"The city next door, Durham, the City of Medicine."

"You must work at Duke Medical Center."

"Not at my age." He smiles again. It seems to lengthen the short creases radiating from the corners of his eyes. "My wife's doctor does. A fine young man, about your age. Forty, forty-five."

"Fifty, thank you." I return the smile.

"A saint, this doctor. I love him. He keeps my wife alive and well. No small accomplishment. You would love him for that, right?"

"Absolutely."

"I love him so much he keeps us from Florida. That's where we thought we'd retire. But a doctor keeps your wife alive and well, you stay. Besides, Chapel Hill is better. A very nice place. Friendly and gracious like New York is not. But a person sees things differently when he has a good reason. You know?"

"Yes, I know. We came here for my wife to go to school. It was her turn to make a change."

"Good, very good." He is nodding from the shoulders again. I can almost feel mine begin. We fall silent and move forward, only two left between the tables and us.

"He keeps my wife with me, this doctor," he repeats, his voice deep in appreciation. "For this I love him."

I slide to the left, avoiding the right branch of the split, and am still beside him. A voice over his shoulder asks, "Sir, could you give me your name and address?"

As he turns another volunteer is waiting for me, a woman topped with a small blue-gray beehive, blue-tinted bifocals, blue eye shadow. A blue woman. I move toward her.

"I'll spell it for you," the old man says. "M-o-s-c-h-o-v-i-t-z, Saul, 1808 South Lake Shore Drive."

"I'll spell it for you," I say to the blue woman before she can ask. The old man, ballot in hand, looks over at me. He waits.

"P-a-s-t-e-r-n-a-k, Louis," I say. "2478 Foxwood Drive." We are practically neighbors. The blue woman peers through the bottom half of her bifocals and flips pages until she finds my name.

"Your ballot, sir," she says. "Thank you for voting."

"Thank you," I say. The man still waits and watches. I think of my father who didn't get to grow old, who never seemed particularly like a Jew, my agnostic, totally assimilated, urbane, sophisticated father. For a flash I miss him terribly again. This man feels every bit as modern, yet more a Jew. For a moment I am a Member of the Tribe. I don't remember having such a strong desire for this. I decide to like it.

"Shall we?" Saul asks. We are going to do this together.

"After you," I say. His smile broadens.

Once again, Saul rocks forward and back. I say to myself he rocked like that on many a Saturday morning at an Orthodox or Conservative synagogue where a cantor sang the ancient rituals in the ancient tongue, no watered down Sunday morning ceremony at a Reform temple like the one I stopped attending as soon as I could, for want of feeling. (I may be wrong now, it has been years, and I was a kid.) He had Bar Mitzvah, I only confirmation, my congregation's capitulation in order to look like everyone else, to fit in. Though in all likelihood I would have tired of his synagogue as I tired of my temple, one thing is sure: I have not been to the spring or drunk from the well like Saul has.

He turns to the left and walks the fifteen feet to the row of black-curtained booths. I follow him until we are side-by-side at two that are empty. He goes to the left, I to the right. At the same moment our left hands reach forward and part the curtains. We turn toward each other and nod a simple acknowledgement. I feel the warmth, but this time from within me as much from him.

He extends a hand.

"Moschovitz," he says with a knowing smile.

"Pasternak," I answer. I reach for his hand, squeeze it, hold it a few extra moments, and then accept that I must let go. With a final nod, almost a bow, we disappear into our booths.

I read the instructions on the ballot and follow them, filling in boxes this time instead of punching holes. There is so much to vote on, so many ballot measures to identify. I try to hurry.

When I come out, Saul is gone. I think about going after him but decide against it. Now the place seems empty, or not a place at all, but I look at the crowd around me. *Shalom,*   I   say,   and   walk   into   the   sunlight.

IN THE MIDDLE

I AWAKENED TO LIFTING FOG and the squawking of Luna's ducks loving the puddles from the night's rain. Through the stairwell rose the crackle of new fire in the woodstove, the thunk of a log as the kindling collapsed under its weight, the clink of steel on steel as Luna returned the lid to its seat on the stove's surface, reminding me that she had learned to love the art of damping the fire to a slow burn and the simple satisfaction of finding a few coals alive in the morning.

Lying there listening, reviewing the night, I thought of the funk Daniel's not coming had put her in. I had gone to bed knowing I had not done enough to help her out of it, yet Luna performed her routines like any morning, respecting the door I leave open for the heat rising up. I had to concentrate to find her hum weaving through the sounds of her chores, and finding it, knew she had recovered. I felt a hint of disappointment.

I had waited up with Luna for Daniel's arrival, watched her pace and stare into the rain, listened, said he'd be there in the morning. I had read her daughter Hannah back to sleep after she awakened from a bad dream. I had made her toast and tea. She was teary, appreciative, appealing.

At midnight I rose from the couch to go to bed. From two steps up the stairs I turned to watch her at the stove not ten feet away. She stood facing it in the quilted robe she had stitched together from random patches of material early in the year she had been renting my back room.

"I'm sorry he hasn't come," I said again.

She pushed her thighs toward the stove, almost

touching it, then clasped her hands behind her, stretching her head and shoulders back so far they seemed poised to meet somewhere behind her. After a long sigh she released her hands and leaned forward over the stove, turning her head in slow circles, first one way, then the other.

"Some father," she said. "Didn't I tell you he wouldn't make it?"

"He'll be here by morning," I said again. "The storm held him up."

"It gave him an excuse to play. The snow level is down to a thousand feet in the Cascades."

"What does that mean?" I asked.

"That he parked his car and strapped on his snow shoes."

"In the night?"

"Midday. He doesn't go out alone at night."

She was sure something had distracted him. Daniel, she once said, was a junkie for severe weather. Chasing swollen rivers rising, gales sweeping the coast, blizzards raging, put three hundred thousand miles of the Northwest roads on his four-wheel drive Subaru.

Before his letter arrived two months before, Luna had spoken of him in mostly harsh tones. "He couldn't find space in his heart for his child and the wilderness at the same time," she once said. A few terse sentences were the customary extent of her remarks about Daniel, but in a year she had revealed the basic facts. In 1976, when Luna was visiting a friend in Bozeman, she saw him reading his poetry in a coffee shop, then bumped into him at a Montana alpine lake. A few months later she moved into his cabin with a view of the Blackfoot, his favorite river. Four months later she was pregnant, and seven months into it she concluded that Daniel wasn't going to make a commitment. She returned to Arcata to have her baby in the home of friends, stayed with them until they had twins, then answered my ad for the big room and private bath on the back side of my first floor.

Luna leaned toward the woodstove but kept an arch in her back, a dancer's pose. Her fine, straight hair skimmed the stove's surface. "I won't get more than a phone call," she said.

"Be careful. You won't like the smell of burning hair."

She straightened up and smiled.

"After four years he decides to meet his daughter but has to pretend he's only a friend," she said, her frown returning. "He wants to watch her from a distance to see what he can do. That's what he said. See what he can do."

"Did he say that in the letter?"

"Yes, and again a few days ago. He had to remind me."

"Maybe this time, when he sees her, it will feel too big for him to drop, like he knows he's running out of time."

With one shake of her head, Luna bounced her mane into place behind her. "Nothing is too big for him to drop. Save for the wilderness and poetry."

"I'm sorry, Luna."

"Not critical anymore, Attorney Frankel?"

"I had questions, not criticisms."

She leaned against the wall next to the stove and folded her arms. "They were more than questions, Will. But you were right about me." She looked down. "I've carried myself away."

She blinked her eyes, held them shut a moment, brushed at one with the back of a hand, then at an errant strand of hair I couldn't see.

"I never said that."

"What did you say?"

I came over to the stove. "That you seem uncertain about what you want, not for Hannah but for yourself."

"Something like that, but harsher."

I had to nod. She was right.

Luna inhaled a big, slow breath through her nose, then sighed hard.

"Will?" Her fingers, long for a small woman, spread wide as daddy long legs and skimmed the surface of the woodstove. Her eyes opened wide.

"Yes?"

"Would you come to bed with me?" she asked. "Just hold me?"

"That is not a good idea."

"We could just hold each other. Can't friends do that?"

Friends, I thought. After a year in my house, "friends" was the word we used to describe what we shared. We had fallen into routines, mostly around Hannah, and seemed to like them. Though Luna had chosen to crowd most of her belongings into her big back room and stashed the rest in the storeroom behind my shop, my home had become theirs. Ours. At meals midway through the year, we made a game of finding the right word to describe us. We laughed at our choices. Roommates, roomies, householders, housemates, insignificant others. None was sufficient, but the night we landed on friends, we mirrored oh-well nods and moved on to some other subject.

Luna turned toward me. "You need attention, too, you distant man. There's a story you've not told me."

My nod surprised me. For more than five years since a bitter divorce ended a short marriage, I had not let myself near a woman, except twice when there was little feeling. I wondered whether in her disappointment and need Luna could lift me from my deep freeze if I would let her try. Our eyes had begun to meet over Hannah's head at dinner, when I looked over the top of my book to find her glancing at me, while she crocheted on the couch, in the midst of shared chores, or when I filled in as Hannah's evening reader. In those moments I would imagine Luna over me, large hungry eyes staring down, silky black hair shrouding me like a curtain, full breasts close, closing. Now, when it shouldn't happen, it could, and I wasn't sure I wanted it for the right reasons, even if there were no Daniel.

"We can comfort each other," she said. "Only that."

"Even if Daniel doesn't show up, how could you want this?"

"This? What do you think *this* is?"

"A different man in your bed than the one you've been dreaming of for the last two months and wanting in your bed tonight."

Pressing her lips together in a firm line, as if hearing something she might not want to answer, Luna removed the stove lid and peered into the fire. The light cast a shimmering glow on her oval face.

"It's wonderful how this stove won't smoke when the lid is off."

"That's how downdraft stoves behave once the fire has lots of coals."

She looked up from the fire with sad eyes I only half wished to see.

"We could just hold each other," she said.

We did. In her bed, with Luna in her flannels and me in my boxers, I curled around her, pulled her to me, wrapped her in my arms. She asked me to hold her tight. When I did she took my hand and held it inches from her mouth. Soft, warm air blew on my fingers in the slowing rhythm of her breath. It felt good, in a stand-alone way, free of expectation. Important.

Hannah slept in her bed by the window. Raindrops pattered like a crowd of tiny, rushing feet on the panes above her. Luna pushed back into me. I swallowed hard, feeling strong and foolish in my restraint, then relaxed my arms and closed my eyes.

"Goodnight, Luna," I said.

"Goodnight, Will."

She fell asleep before I did, but not by much. The sleep that came over me remained so light that even the rain ceasing awakened me. Or was it the ducks squabbling with each other or reacting to the sound of a car coming down Highway 101 from the north, from Oregon? The latter sound worried me, and my worry grew when Luna stirred and pushed into me, tightening our fetal curve. She opened my hand and pulled it to her breasts, then purred and rolled over, snuggling her body close to mine, tucking her head under my chin and folding her arms against my chest. I waited a few minutes and turned away. After another, she cupped herself around me from behind and put a hand on my hip.

"Are you awake?" she whispered.

I didn't answer. She took in a long, deep breath, then let out a strong one that seemed to relax her even more. She moved her hand to my shoulder.

When her hand became heavy, I slid out of her bed, picked up my clothes, found my way in the darkness to my own. I couldn't remember dreaming. Then the warming sun, the squawking ducks, the smell of coffee, quiet footfalls. Little girl's feet padding on the living room rug. Sandals clopping on kitchen tiles. Boots clunking in from the back hall, and a harmonized good morning, male and female together, with warm, throaty grumbles and hints of laughter.

Daniel.

"WOULD A FEW CHANGES be okay?" Luna had asked over coffee at the kitchen counter a few mornings after Daniel's letter arrived. It had swept her into dreaminess, her bitterness disappearing in a bloom of preparation. Her eyes scanned the living room, then around the dining corner, then behind her to the outer wall of the kitchen.

"Curtains for the kitchen window?" she asked in the high-pitched voice I took for doubt. "A cheery tablecloth? Maybe a few other things?"

"Sure," I said.

Only a week passed before lacy white curtains framed the window, and a dark blue tablecloth with yellow daisies covered my scarred oak family treasure. Soon Luna asked with unnecessary care to put a wicker rocker by the front window. I tried to acknowledge her ambivalence with a big smile and nearly pulled it off. She turned away. Next, a wooden floor lamp with a lathe-turned base and an etched paper shade found a home between the couch and my easy chair, and later still a ceramic pitcher with swirling pastel curves took a place on the stone mantel I had built behind the woodstove. Last, a red straw hearth brush with a branch for a handle leaned against the mantel. I wondered why these items had not appeared before.

"What other beautiful things do you have in the storeroom?"

"Oh, more than you would want in here, Will. My things would take over, if I brought them all in. Some other time, maybe, a few more."

Luna dove into springtime projects and worked at them alone, as if I should not help prepare my house for another man. On weekends, when I found time to work in my shop, I would look through its open door to find her tending new potted plants on the patio and in the greenhouse, watering, transplanting, pruning. Sometimes I found myself helping with projects she initiated, but mostly I watched, and Luna watched my watching. The pleasure we had taken for granted in our routines became a fragile, threatened gift we had exchanged but never acknowledged and now could not. Her feminine touch was not for us, whatever we were, but for Hannah and Daniel and herself. In nearly the same breath she seemed impulsive and restrained, effusive and self-conscious. I filled up with questions I didn't ask, but more than that, I felt a growing sense of loss and believed that Luna did, too.

A week before Daniel arrived, on a rainy Saturday afternoon that kept us inside, I brought him up for the first time. Hannah was sleeping away a cold, and Luna was in her rocker repairing my grandmother's afghan. Months before, she had removed it from the back of the couch because, she said, the holes from years of stretching it over the tips of toes threatened its future. She had found an almost perfect match for its cranberry and gray colors. Her flurry of nesting for Daniel had put an end to the project, but on that Saturday, comfortable with her preparations, it was back in her hands.

"The new yarn will fade and match this fine old thing even better," she said. "I'll make it strong." In that one sitting she mastered its intricate pattern. The scattering of holes began to disappear.

"When Daniel arrives should I be less fatherly?" I asked from my stool at the counter. I had never referred to myself that way, nor had Luna.

She looked up from the couch. "I'm not going to protect Daniel from you."

"It might be easier for Hannah."

"For you to back away would be harder for her. Besides, Daniel should see what you do. You're not Hannah's father, you're not even a father, but you do all the right things."

"I didn't know that."

"We haven't talked about these things," she said, keeping her eyes on her work.

"Are you going to tell her that Daniel is her father?"

"It depends. If Daniel..." She looked out the window. "Hannah deserves this chance. So does Daniel, but he will have to do more than watch."

I rose from the stool, went to the kitchen sink, and looked out the window. "I have a role in this?"

"You are the steadiest person Hannah's going to have through this."

I turned and leaned against the sink. "What exactly will *this* be?"

Luna stared. "What, exactly, are you implying?"

"From the way you are dressing up this place, I'd say this visit is about more than Hannah."

Luna stopped running her hook through the yarn. A long silence stretched out before she looked up.

"This visit is about Hannah," she said.

"Are you going to hide the truth that your lover is her father?"

Luna lay the hook and afghan beside her on the couch, rose, and started for the hallway door. "Is this cross-examination?"

I laced my hands behind my head and crossed one leg over the other. "Hannah needs your steadiness more than mine."

She turned. "Is that all you are concerned about?"

I pushed my glasses tight against my eyes and stroked the spine of my nose. "I haven't figured that out yet."

We stared at each other, uncertain what faces to wear.

"I want to give this a chance, Will. It's a lot to ask of you."

I worked my lower teeth against my upper lip and nodded.

"Please don't change while Daniel is here," she said. "Hannah won't understand."

"What about you? Are you going to change?"

She turned away, left the kitchen, and closed the door behind her.

"MORNING, HANNAH," I said, stopping to tweak her toes with mine. She was on her back on the living room floor looking from her mother at the door to Daniel in my easy chair.

"Hi," she answered, closing her eyes, something she had not done before when greeting me.

Daniel, one hand extended as he approached me and a book in the other as he rose, wore an apologetic smile, his blue eyes searching mine for what I took to be acceptance of his being here. Yet he appeared sure of himself. I wondered if he expected the things he wanted to come to him. I tried to answer "yes" with my eyes as I reached down for Hannah with one hand, tilting her up toward a hug. Her dead weight suggested she didn't want up. With the other I shook Daniel's hand as I straightened up. His grip was firm, and he held it.

"Thanks for having me here," he began. "I won't wear out my welcome." With a sheepish grin he glanced down toward Hannah for the smallest part of a second. "Hannah won't let me."

On the cover of the book he held, a whitewater river ran through forested mountains.

"Not to worry," I said, letting go of his hand and waving off his concern. "Stay as long as you...need to. What's your book?"

"*A River Runs Through It.*"

"Daniel's most recent bible," Luna said from the door, drawing a double take from him. She noticed this, stopped packing the basket at her feet, and moved toward him. "You've read it how many times?" She put her hand in his.

"This is the third," he said, smiling. "Probably not the last."

"I have a few bibles of my own," I said. "Do you recommend it?"

"Yes, if you believe everyone loses grace and needs the rest of his life to find it. And that some don't."

Luna let go of Daniel's hand and fixed her eyes on me.

"So, today's a picnic for the three of you?" I asked.

"Hannah is going to visit the twins." Luna said. "Daniel and I are going to the beach."

"I'm gonna go to Sam and April's," Hannah mumbled through her thumb.

"You'll have fun with those sillies." I looked up at Daniel. "Does the story propose a way?"

"It's short. More like a novella. You could read it by dinner," Daniel said.

Hannah rolled to her side. I winked at her and gained a smile. Luna left Daniel's side and went to an overloaded laundry basket on the floor by the front door, some of its contents spilling as she lifted it. She called out to me over her shoulder as she started for her car, her voice raised an octave. "Will, could you take the lasagna from the fridge by five?"

I shouted after her that I wouldn't forget.

"Will you be in your shop?" Daniel asked. "I took a peek. It looks like an old-time blacksmith's shop."

"For a while," I answered. "I'm only a weekend dilettante."

Luna was outside now, loading things into the car.

"Daniel," she called out, "Will you help me?"

We went to the door. Daniel picked up the items that had dropped out of the basket and went to the car. Luna passed him on her way back to get Hannah.

At the door, she stopped for a moment, a frown on her face. "Here's a little something for you," she said. She stuffed a gray sock in my pants pocket.

"From the floor by my bed," she whispered. "I think Daniel saw it."

"Big mistake," I said.

"You'll be here for dinner, Daddy Will?"

Luna and I stared at each other in disbelief, but her eyes guided mine back to Hannah. "Sure will, Hannah," I said. "See you then, okay?"

She didn't answer, but my smile got one in return. Luna stepped inside, reached down, and hauled her daughter to her feet. Hannah reached up with her arms, but Luna would have none of carrying her and offered only her hand. They held hands all the way to the car.

From the doorway I watched Luna and Daniel putting in the last items and closing up the car. In the backseat the neck of a bottle of wine and a bottle of juice punched above a bag of apples and oranges, a loaf of bread, and the tin Luna used for cookies. Daniel, arms folded, watched Luna strap their daughter into the car seat behind him. In a few minutes they were backing out from under the broad canopy of the giant cedar from which I had hung an inner tube for Hannah. Luna laughed at something Daniel must have said. She gave him a quick kiss, then looked back toward the house with a smile and a wave. Hannah, thumb still poking into her mouth, seemed to be staring at me, but her gaze went to the sky. I wondered if she already needed to find the protection that escape provides. Then they were rolling down the hill toward the ramp to Highway 101.

THROUGH THE OPEN ROLLING DOOR of my shop I saw Daniel ambling around from the front side of the house, the sun low behind him. My attention had been on the piece heating in the coal fire of the forge. A steel bar three eighths of an inch thick, three inches wide, and forty-eight inches long was becoming a pot rack for the kitchen, a house gift to match Luna's touches. Waiting, I cranked on the blower, fanning the fire with a blast of air. In less than a minute the steel was yellow again, ready to bend the finial ends of the finished bar into a C-shape to provide surfaces for the bolts that would hold the rack to studs in the kitchen wall. Then I remembered that I had not located the studs on the wall I would mount it on. Shaking my head, I pulled the piece from the fire, picked up the hammer and began the bend on the far side of the anvil.

"Your anvil rings when you strike it. Not in this heat when you're bending, but earlier, when you were striking hard."

Daniel was leaning on the doorframe.

"A good ring is supposed to mean a good anvil," I said with mock authority.

"It's just a myth?"

I laid the piece on the forge and my hammer on the anvil, grabbed a poker, and broke up the fire, scattering fragments of coke along the surface of the forge, and laid the poker aside.

"I once sold an anvil cheap because it had no ring. To a real blacksmith. He told me it was awful quiet, so I figured I wouldn't get a dollar a pound. Of course, I didn't. At a fair a year later he told me it was the best anvil he ever had. Smiled when he said it."

"You were laughing when I came in. It reminded me of moments discovering the right words for a poem, or a trout's first true tug on the line, the tug the tells you you've got it."

"Nothing so perfect happened. I just remembered I hadn't determined the exact location for this."

"You'll figure it out. Or Luna will."

I removed my leather apron and hung it over the anvil's horn, then went to the faucet to clean my hands.

"Luna wants me to remind you not to make yourself scarce at dinner on our account," Daniel said, moving closer to the anvil. "She thinks you might."

I suppressed a chuckle at how much was behind her remark that Daniel could not know, then remembered that he might have formed an impression I hoped Luna had tried to correct.

"That's why I'm stopping. If there's time after I shower, I'll help."

"She would rather you not."

"Okay by me," I said. "You left your book for me. Maybe I'll start it."

"So, you're a lawyer."

"You could say that."

"Then this must be what you love."

"That's quite an assumption, but not inaccurate." I dried my hands on a clean rag, taking time for a more thoughtful response. "Do you know the Robert Frost poem in which he says, 'For only when love and need are one, and work is play for mortal stakes....'"

"'Is the deed ever really done for Heaven and the future's sakes.' That's from 'Two Tramps In Mudtime.'"

"I don't expect to be that lucky," I said. "Like I said this morning, I'm a dilettante."

"I'm more optimistic. Or selfish. What kind of a lawyer are you?"

"General practice. People, small businesses, pro bono work for nonprofits, disability, too much domestic, and a bit of criminal, unfortunately. And I'm a judge for the tribal court in Hoopa."

Daniel sat on the edge of the water tank. "How's the child custody stuff?"

"A dirty job that has to be done. I think I've been chosen."

"It must be tough to get between parents over a child."

"I'd rather get between them and help them settle than believe one is right and tear the skin off the other. But if I tried settling every case, I'd piss off the ones paying me."

He nodded and smiled. "I should go before this gets too interesting. Luna wants my help."

"One question. Isn't that book you are reading about a young man who lives in a state of perfection when his hands are on a rod and reel? Somebody told me that."

"It's about grace. Maybe that's the same as perfection. But his life is a serious mess. It's like he is blessed by God when he is fishing and caught by the Devil when he's not. But the book is not just about him. It's about his family, too, and much more than that. It's about words. You would like it."

"Forge welds are perfect moments, if you do everything just right. Turning two pieces of steel into one with only fire, hammer and anvil. When it works, I feel blessed, as if I've been given a taste of perfection. I suppose that's grace. It's more possible in here than any other place I've found."

A hint of a smile crossed Daniel's face, a smile of understanding. "No interest in a scientific explanation of how a weld works?"

I returned his smile. "People discovered how to weld two pieces of steel together long before there was science to explain it."

His smile became a grin that filled his face. He jammed his hands into his jeans pockets and went off toward the house. I went to the shop door to watch him go, thinking I could like this man and wondering why my errant sock was not a strike against me. Perhaps it was, and I was just naïve. Luna, standing at the back door, said "Hi, Will" almost below hearing, then greeted Daniel with a hug and a kiss. I saw only his back and her hands. For the longest time.

HANNAH LAY IN HER PAJAMAS on the floor, eyes on the ceiling, rocking back and forth, sucking hard on her thumb. A bowl of chicken soup waited on the table, with Luna to one side of it. She hadn't been able to keep her daughter there for more than a few spoonsful. I was in my easy chair, just beginning *A River Runs Through It*. Daniel stood at the counter lacing French bread with garlic butter.

"Okay, sweetie, if you aren't going to eat Will's soup from last night, it's bedtime."

"You and Daddy Will take me."

"Let's you and I read *The Wind in the Willows*. Will and Daniel need time to talk. They're just getting to know each other."

Hannah shrugged as her mother dragged her to her feet and led her to the couch. I went to the counter and stood across from Daniel as he wrapped the bread in aluminum foil.

"Tell me about the story," I said.

Luna looked up from settling with Hannah on the couch and finding their page.

"Okay, but not much. Small town Montana preacher raises two sons on equal amounts of religion and fly fishing. He has more faith in the fly fishing, though he'd never say that to a parishioner. For him it's closer to where God might be found, but he can't tell his flock that church is not the best place to look. The younger son is the best fly fisherman his father and older brother have ever seen, as close to perfect as can be, but when he's not in a river, the kid's a drinking, partying, gambling, drugging, womanizing, brawling wild man bent on self-destruction. When the father and older brother watch him fish, they believe they see perfect grace bestowed by God upon the family disgrace. He seems to survive anything, but they are afraid for him. The boy is a hopeless contradiction, beauty and the beast."

Daniel took the garlic bread to the stove and opened the oven door.

"No! Not yet!" Luna cried out.

"The lasagna looks ready, Lun."

"It's not. I'll tell you when."

"Sure."

Luna closed the book and lifted her daughter into her arms. "We'll finish reading in our room. You've got things sort of in order. Say good night to Will and Daniel, Hannah."

"Ga night, Daddy Will."

"Is that all you're going to say?"

Hannah laid her head leaned on her mother's shoulder and closed her eyes. "Ga night."

"Come on, sweetie, ga night who?"

Luna came to the counter. Daniel placed his hand on Hannah's back so lightly she might not have felt it. "It's okay, Hannah. Good night."

In a few steps they were at the door to the back hall, then gone, shutting it behind them.

"So," I continued. "Is it hopeful or despairing?"

"Read it." He smiled. "It's not much more than a hundred pages."

I took the salad to the table and fetched the wine. Daniel and I sat at opposite ends. We talked about fishing, poetry and blacksmithing. When the door to the back opened, he kept on until he saw my eyes shift away from him and not return. Luna had gone to the oven and was taking out the dish of lasagna. She put it on the stovetop.

"This needs to sit for a few minutes," she said. Coming to the table, she poured herself a glass of wine.

"Here's our story," she began. "I saw this man reading poetry in a diner in Bozeman when I was visiting. I liked his poems and the way he read, like each one was a little play. We kept looking at each other while he was waiting for his turn. He was the last to read, and after that we didn't say a word, so I never expected to see him again."

She paused and looked over the top of her glasses, perhaps wanting Daniel to take the next part of the story. He only smiled.

"Two days later we bumped into each other at a lake in....what's that place called?"

"The Bitterroot Range," Daniel said. He straightened up and wiped his lips with his napkin.

"What was the name of that place, Daniel?"

"The Bitterroots," he said, his voice raised a pitch.

"No. Where you read."

"Dimple's Diner. A transformed Mobil station that still pumps gas. You eat in the office and two car bays. The last two bays are the kitchen. No service for cars. Just pumps."

"That's it. He walked into my campsite at sunset with a big moon coming up behind the lake. Dropped his pack and stayed for dinner."

"By invitation," Daniel added.

"That lake was such a sweet place," Luna said, her eyes wide with memory. She touched Daniel's forearm. "You liked the river better."

"The outlet stream had a long, deep hole about a hundred yards down, under a bluff."

"You fried trout," Luna said. "With your fish we stretched two days' food into four."

Daniel nodded summarily, as if the subject had been exhausted and the praise was enough.

Luna continued. "We ate on that flat rock by the water and laid our bags there for the night."

Daniel crossed his knife and fork upon his empty plate. He dabbed his lips with his napkin and refilled our wine glasses.

"I wouldn't mind watching you in your forge one day. Maybe I could help," he said.

"Don't think about Daniel helping until I've had enough of him," Luna said. She rose and went to the counter, kissing the top of his neat blond hair on the way.

"If you do some big work, I could strike for you." He smiled. "I mean later."

"I've done that!" Luna shouted from the counter, where she cradled a peach pie in her hands. "I stood on the opposite side of the anvil with a sledge hammer. He hit little tapping blows to show me where to hit hard. I didn't move much steel."

"Your shop is pretty low tech," Daniel said. "Your only compromise is that power hammer."

"I've seen him use two strikers at once. It's a dance."

"The Big Guy moves a lot more steel than even three strikers could," I said, "and he's safer. After you've used The Big Guy, strikers are only for show."

"But using strikers is such a dance." Luna sighed. "Especially with two. Like when Dan and Flint helped you."

I smiled. "It can be when you shut out everything else. But two long-handled sledge hammers flying at the same time is scary."

Luna cut three pieces of pie. She went to the refrigerator and returned with vanilla ice cream.

Daniel crossed his arms and looked at Luna. "I've seen it but not done it. I'd like to."

"Not tomorrow," Luna said, fixing her gaze at me. "We've planned our day with Hannah."

"That's fair enough," Daniel said. "Will, do you ever take off work early? Like maybe Monday?"

"I could do that."

"Hhh," Luna said. She scooped ice cream onto two pieces of pie and went to the couch without the third. Choosing the side nearest the easy chair, she picked up my old afghan from her basket on the rug between them. Tucking her legs under her, she began spidering the crochet hook through the yarn, but her fingers stopped, and she gazed off to some far away place like Hannah had when they left in the morning. I thought of the dark picture she had painted of Daniel before his letter arrived, and of the low glow that brightened that picture the few times a fond memory broke through. The letter had come like the first true day of spring, the one you think you can count on. After that, Luna had stayed bright except for the night he arrived so late.

She dimmed the lamp she had placed between the couch and the easy chair and sank down into the plush of its cushions. In just a day she seemed to be losing that brightness, as if her time with Daniel had already taken a bad turn.

Luna knew I was watching her. Daniel did, too. I wondered did she feel as exposed as I did.

IN A DREAM TOWARD MORNING, I saw Daniel standing in hip waders in the swift shallows of a sparkling stream. He cast his line across the rushing water toward a still, dark pool under a bluff on the far side. He cast again and again, each time arching his back and whipping his arm forward in a single motion free of hesitation at the moment of transition from going back to coming forward. Each cast took the same shape as the one before but with more or less energy as he changed the force, the arc, the distance.

I moved to the edge of the stream to better watch him. Time seemed to stop, as if catching a fish no longer mattered. After each cast, he took another step from the shallows into the deeper, stronger current between himself and the pool, anchoring himself as he pushed closer to the outer edge of easy water. A few times he looked over his shoulder with an adolescent grin that seemed to say that the real fun waits to start until the risks begin. Before each move into deeper water he stared upstream and down, seeming to measure the current, planning his escape, should it come to that. Sometimes he looked back at me with that same grin, but smaller, and with a question, like a kid.

Luna sat nearby in the sunlight on a flat boulder at the water's edge, knees drawn up, arms draped around her shins, one hand clasping tight to the other wrist, statue-still, staring past Daniel toward the still pool. I looked there and noticed my reflection next to his on the dark surface. We were smiling, but I didn't like it and turned away, the willed act of a conscious dreamer. I pulled myself out of the dream and struggled back to sleep.

A SLANT OF MORNING SUNLIGHT framed Luna standing at my door in her patchwork robe. I saw her through filmy eyes as I rolled from my side to my back. Except for the day she came to check out the place, she had not been in my room. My surprise at seeing her there must have shown. She excused herself with a polite bow.

"Okay that I opened your door?" she asked. "You can't smell the bacon when it's closed."

"Thanks. I smell it now. What time is it?"

"Nine," she said, her voice carrying an edge. "Late for you. Why did you close the door?"

"To protect your privacy."

"We don't need to change our routines." She smiled a wistful smile and gazed at the sunlight beaming in the east window, then out toward the shining trees to the west. "Breakfast is almost ready. Will you join us?"

"If you'll just leave pronto, I'll jump right up."

Luna smiled a real smile, though still wistful. "Fair enough," she said. Folding her arms and taking a last glance around, she turned and left, her sandals clacking down the stairs.

MINUTES LATER, Daniel straightened up from the oven with a plate of pancakes in his hand. He moved to the counter and piled on the last cakes from the griddle.

"Hannah," he called out as he carried the plate to the table. He sounded like an actor unsure of his lines. "They're hot."

Hannah rolled to her tummy and crawled turtle-slow toward us on her knees and one hand. The other kept a thumb in her mouth.

"Get up, big girl," Luna whispered. "Get those pancakes while they're hot."

Hannah stayed on her hands and knees all the way to my corner of the table. Luna glanced at me with a pleading face that perplexed me until I looked at her daughter, whose eyes spoke to me, not to her mother. I picked her up and, rising from my chair, hugged her, then moved to the chair opposite Luna and put Hannah at the end of the table. Daniel watched from the other.

Playing father to Hannah seemed right and wrong and left me wondering if Daniel might make a better try if I insisted on making myself scarce, but it was too late.

AFTER BREAKFAST, a warm April sun drew us to the back patio and settled us into the lawn chairs. The ocean, rolling in the distance like an endless blue prairie, mirrored the first true calm I felt since Friday night. Hannah retrieved her three-wheeler from the back hallway and weaved slow figure eights around us, silent but unabashed at watching us. Each time she passed she flicked at my pant leg with the fingers of her free hand. We were quiet, lacking even the small talk of breakfast, and all but Hannah came close to dozing.

"I liked watching you fish," I said, flushing red as soon as the words were out.

Luna and Daniel looked at each other, then back at me.

"You must have been dreaming." Luna's voice was breathy and filled with sweetness.

"Yes, I suppose I was."

In the awkward silence that followed, Hannah got off her three-wheeler and leaned against my chair, reminding me of my old cat, Lefty, who would come down from the top of the refrigerator to settle into the lap of the person who most needed attention. She skimmed her fingers over the hair on my forearms, a recent habit I liked for the smooth tingle it gave my skin and the simple fact that she did it. I stroked her hair just once, enough to get a smile. She backpedaled to her mother, took her hand, and placed it on her hair for her mother to stroke.

"You needn't explain, Will," Daniel said, his voice quiet and reassuring. "Maybe it's symbolic of something important for you to think about."

"I would rather ask another question about the book," I said, to change the subject.

"Okay, but just one," Daniel said.

"We'll see if he can be brief," said Luna.

"Don't worry, Will. I won't give it away."

"The father feels ambivalent about preaching, that's for sure. Reminds me of going to synagogue to hear Rabbi Hirsch's sermons. Only when he turned to nature did he get truly excited. I thought he should take us out of the synagogue and into Forest Park. That's in St. Louis. Of course he never did. But my father did. And into the Ozarks. I never got enough of it. It seems the boys in the story get enough, but it doesn't necessarily make a difference."

"What's your question?"

"I'm not sure. Something about the father's passion for words and his difficulty accepting their limitations. He talks about that. Must be tough on a preacher. Most people want words to set them straight. But finding them in nature? Isn't nature a place to escape words?"

"The father loves words as much as fly fishing. He believes words are living things we try to find when we are stuck. It's in our nature to create problems for ourselves and ponder them, searching for words that will set us straight. He hasn't much faith in the book he's bound to preach from, which he knows contains the words of men, not God. I think he wants to believe a person can find more helpful ones in nature. He says you can find them under stones in the river. Maybe he hopes that being there empties you and clears out a space for the right words to come. What better place than a wild river to wash away everything that gets in the way? So he makes his boys fly fish as often as he makes them go to church. I suppose he thinks that from one you get only discipline, he's big on discipline, but from the other you get discipline and emptiness, silence, discovery. Of course, they prefer fishing. The father and the older brother really want the experience to save the younger one. Appealing, isn't it?"

He looked at Luna. "And I didn't tell him the story."

"You said more than I'd want to hear."

"He asked, Luna."

Hannah made another circuit and stopped behind Daniel.

"I would think he might use fly fishing as a metaphor in his sermons like he does with his sons," I said.

"He's a realist. He's giving the congregation what it wants, something simple, and hoping for the best. If he tells them to go fly fishing, they'll think he's crazy. They are working too hard to have time for metaphors."

"You might be selling them short."

Daniel smiled. "Hmmh. Well, aren't we all limited in some ways?"

"Yes," Luna said emphatically. "But does he really think the right words can be found in those dark pools? Under stones?"

"I'm just giving you my interpretation. He believes that the motion of the cast mimics nature's rhythms and slows you down, lets you see the beauty that gets lost in concerns. Practicing something like that is your best chance. You know, we always cast into the darkest pools, the hardest places to see. Maybe the words are there, or in the struggle. It's not intellectual or rational, and you won't find them by listening to anybody else."

"I suppose we never find the words that will put us at rest," Luna said. "We find something we want, then make up words to persuade us it is what we want it to be before we know if it really is."

"Hmmmh," Daniel said, smiling, showing his perfect teeth, deepening his dimples and the premature crow's feet in his otherwise smooth face. "Hmmmh," he repeated.

I could understand Luna still wanting this man who struggled against being father to their child. He was luminous and warm in a distant but reachable way. He had an inquiring mind and loved to say what he thought he had grasped. I decided he knew himself for what he was, with all the walls and gaps that Luna spoke of.

"Maybe you get a taste of grace," he said, "of being blessed, no matter how..." He paused. "No matter how else you are. The possibility of salvation, of elevating yourself above your limitations. The father wants that desperately for his kid because he sees him going down. He lives so straight but never feels blessed like his son seems to be when a fly rod is in his hand."

"If the boy could watch himself fish," said Luna. "And watch himself not fish, he might see the difference. It might save him. I haven't read the book, but just listening, from what you are saying, it seems like that's what his father wants him to do."

Daniel chuckled. "Funny reading group. We're talking about a book one of us hasn't finished and another hasn't read."

With that he rose from his chair and stretched. He turned to Hannah and patted the top of her head as lightly as he might a sucked-dry eggshell you're about to paint for Easter. Hannah frowned, then turned to look toward something in the yard. She allowed him to continue, and he did, with the uncertain look of one who does not know what comes next. As he stood above her, patting and looking down at her, Hannah began to peddle toward me at a furious pace.

"It's not the only thing that's funny about us," he said. "You can finish the book today and still have time for that." He pointed to my shop.

I rose from my chair. "No shop today. It pulls me on the weekends, but today is different. I don't know why, but it is."

Luna got up and hurried inside. Daniel leaned over and looked down at his feet, but I saw his grin. "You know why. She doesn't want us in your shop or even talking about it, you think?"

I chuckled. "Not until she's had enough of you. What else is funny about us?"

"All the ties that cross and bind here." He looked up. "I'd say it's a bit of a knot."

I thought of the sock, but before I could even imagine an answer, Luna returned and sidled in between us. Hannah, on her feet now, bumped against my leg. Luna's face bore the barest smile, warm like the woodstove when it's down to coals. She laced the fingers of one hand into Daniel's, leaving the other behind her. "I'm going to take a shower. The three of you can entertain each other."

She handed Hannah a book, then glided toward the back door, leaving her daughter between her father and me. Hannah grabbed my leg with one hand and looked up at me. With the other she held up *The Wind in the Willows*.

"Read about the possible," Luna said, looking over her shoulder.

DANIEL WATCHED US READ from the dinner table, his fingers knitted behind his head, his legs spread wide. Hannah sat close to me on the couch, schoolgirl straight, hands folded in her lap, eyes fixed on the page. The return of a relied-upon routine did not bring her all the way back to being four years old.

Four or five short chapters sped by with Daniel watching us through most of it before Luna was there, wiping the counters, suggesting it was time to go. He mumbled something about changing shoes and stood up. *A River Runs Through It* lay on the lamp stand. I finished a chapter and closed it, relieved to have an end to being watched at something Daniel seemed unable to appreciate.

"Is it the beach again for you guys?" I asked. The "yes" came from Hannah, with her first delight. They would drive to Patrick's Point, Luna said, then to Big Lagoon, and end with an early dinner at The Seacape in Trinidad. Hannah, she said, loved the fish and chips. It occurred to me for the first time that I had never been to a beach with Luna or Hannah.

As soon as they left, I returned to *A River Runs Through It*. The pages flew by and wrapped me in a story of beauty and ugliness as if I had never paid attention to the way those opposites can inhabit the same space at the same time. I finished in a single sitting.

In the silence I thought of my shop and wanted to go there but remembered saying that it would be a bad idea. Leaning back against the couch and closing my eyes, I saw the three of us on the river like in the dream, but Hannah was there, too, sitting in the sand beneath the boulder on which her mother sat cross-legged. When a dream state started to wash over me, I gave in and followed.

At first nothing changed but for Hannah being there. She played alone in the sand, kicking it with her feet, squeezing it through her fingers, head down. At last she stopped and looked at each of us, for the longest time at Daniel. In water past his waist, fighting the current, his arm cocked for a cast, he paused and looked back as if he had felt our concern. He grabbed the line and secured it to the reel. Looking disappointed, he backed out of the difficult water and plodded toward Hannah.

"Daddy Will?"

"Let him sleep," Luna whispered, but her voice carried a sharp edge. "Come climb up on a stool while your hot chocolate's warming up."

"Mama, I want Daddy Will...."

"Not now, honey. Come away from him. Let him sleep."

"It's okay," I said. "I'm awake. What time is it?"

Luna came to the couch and sat on its edge, her warmth against my leg. She lifted Hannah into her lap. "Ten to three." Her voice squeezed out like drips from a small hole in a dam. "We're back early. Can I ask a big favor?"

"Sure."

"Will you go off somewhere with Hannah?"

I put my hand on her leg. Surprised and embarrassed, I withdrew it right away. "Are you okay?"

"Just for a few hours."

"Yes," I said, rising.

IN THE CAR, hoping to shake off her faraway look, I asked Hannah where she wanted to go.

"For what?" she asked from her car seat. I had secured her in it with surprising ease.

"For whatever you want." We were heading south toward Arcata on 101.

She perked up. "Your office. I wanna see it."

"It's a deal."

Hannah's perk lasted only a moment. As we passed Clam Beach, she found the clouds over the rim of the ocean, and her thumb found its way to her mouth. Then came two questions that unsettled me.

"Do you know Daniel is my daddy?"

"Yes, I know that."

"Does it mean I'm gonna leave our house?"

"I don't know. What does your mama say?"

"She wants us to be a family with Daniel."

"That's a good idea."

"No it isn't," she mumbled through her thumb, her eyes cast downward until she turned back toward the line of great clouds piling high over the water.

I DROVE BY THE MINOR. 101 Dalmatians was due to begin at four. I called Luna from my office.

"Please take her," she said, her voice stiff with control. "I can't thank you enough. Can you bring takeout? A pizza maybe. I'll make a salad."

"I'll bring pizza and a salad," I said. "I can pick it up around five forty-five. Will you call Al Capone's?"

"Could you call before the movie?"

"Hannah wants previews. We've got to hustle. I'll be there by six fifteen. You're okay?"

"By six fifteen," she answered, her voice trembling. I imagined her eyes as sad as they were on Friday night as she stood by the woodstove. She sniffed through a runny nose, then hung up the phone.

LUNA OPENED THE BACKDOOR to take Hannah from the car seat. She had been sweeping the stones of the path to the house. "Did she make it through the movie?" she asked.

"Yup. Loved it. Fell asleep before we got out of Arcata."

I stood by the car while Luna unstrapped her daughter from the car seat.

She looked up from clicking open the straps. "Will you help us?"

"What happened?"

"Please answer my question."

"I have few skills for this, and I'm not impartial about either of you."

She gathered Hannah into her arms. "That should keep things even."

"It's not that simple, Luna. Has Daniel agreed?"

"I don't know what I'm doing. And yes." Her face was gray, her eyes red. "Maybe you can get us to the other side of this in a better way."

"Sounds like you know where it's going." I paused.

Luna's eyes searched my face from behind the shield of her daughter. "I don't know where it's going. Do what you think is right, but go now. I need a minute out here with my daughter."

She turned away.

DANIEL SAT AT THE COUNTER reading the Sunday paper. He looked up but said nothing, then pulled his lips into a tight line. I nodded, and he returned it.

"Are you okay with this?" I asked.

"Well, let's see," he said with a failing smile. "There's the obvious connection you and I have. Literature, love of our avocations, the search for grace in flawed lives. You're troubled by my difficulty with the father role, but you have trouble with Luna's mothering, too. What do you think so far?"

"Keep going."

"Her intensity probably puts you off, and I suppose you find her less than objective. Then there's the sock you left by her bed and the warm sheets and dented pillow. I'm guessing that you're unsure of yourself when it comes to women. You've suffered some damage there, too. So you like both of us, in different ways of course, but you're critical of us, too. And wary. That puts you right in the middle."

"That's almost persuasive. Did she tell you how the sock got there?"

"I believe what she told me," Daniel said. "The innocence of it."

"Thanks for that. Maybe you're already out the door, and this doesn't matter."

"Not really. Give me some credit for being here."

The door opened. With Hannah in her arms, Luna walked between us to the hallway door, fixing her eyes on me. "This child is awake enough for dinner, but she won't stay that way for long. She's escaping. Then maybe you can help us."

OVER WARMED-UP PIZZA, damp salad, and soggy garlic bread we made small talk for a drowsy child until Luna took Hannah to their room to read her to sleep. It wouldn't take long. Daniel found a spot on the end of the couch away from the lamp and the easy chair, leaving open the spaces he must have felt were Luna's and mine. He closed his eyes.

I settled into the easy chair and picked up *A River Runs Through It*, thinking it might help me find a way into the middle, with equal distance on either side. That's not an easy place for a lawyer trained to represent. It occurred to me that I ought to talk with each of them privately first to see what each wanted, feel out how they felt about me playing the neutral role, take some time to examine that for myself. Luna wasn't giving me that chance, and Daniel seemed to be going along for the ride. I thought maybe so was I.

I closed the book and looked at Daniel sitting erect on the couch, staring out the window. What was he thinking, I wondered. Was he deep within himself, pondering some darkness, waiting for some clarified emptiness in which the right words would appear? I saw someone I would like to know. Were the circumstances different, I could imagine us becoming friends.

Opening the book, I began flipping through the pages with my forefinger but gave up quickly. I would define grace for myself. Unusual blessedness falling unevenly and serendipitously from somewhere, I thought. With no explanation for its random distribution. Might it be a quality one could summon from within? Could Daniel, fascinated by its mystery but, as far as I could tell, disengaged from its pursuit except as an abstraction? Could Luna, trapped by driving needs? Could I, so long keeping at bay the kind of forces that were making a wreck of her?

Then Luna was there.

I expected her to sit at the counter or stand by the woodstove, removed from us, but she sat statue-stiff on the far end of the couch from Daniel and folded her hands in her lap. Her eyes darted between us. Daniel turned to face me, leaning forward with his forearms on his thighs and his hands knitted in a listener's pose.

"So, I'll just direct traffic and keep out of the way," I began. "Luna, I think it's fair for you to start because you asked for this."

Luna raised her eyebrows. "I thought maybe you would, I don't know, ask questions."

"Okay. For starters, what's the most important thing you want Daniel to really hear? Then Daniel can answer that, too. Let's see what happens with that."

She shrugged. "This is too hard." I could see her fighting back tears.

"This is what you wanted," Daniel said. "Don't back out now."

"Please don't tell me what to do."

"I'm sorry. I should have said please."

"Say it to me first, Luna," I said. "If that's easier."

She took a deep breath and wriggled tension from her shoulders. "Daniel didn't come here to see what he could do with Hannah. He came here to convince himself of what he can't do. Otherwise he would try something with her. Anything. But he's tried nothing. And he wants me for a lover."

Daniel drew his back up straight but kept his hands knitted, seeming to gather himself together. "I haven't tried much with Hannah, but she hasn't wanted me to. That's plain as day. As for the lover thing, that began with you."

"It takes two, Daniel. As for Hannah, it's your obvious disinterest that keeps her away." She huffed in as if air were scarce. "She needed to know you care right from the start. You backed away as soon as she knew who you were. Even before. You never invited her to know you, but she sees you wanting me. She feels left out. And as for the lover thing, what a lovely name to give what we have shared."

"She sees you wanting me, turning your attention toward me, putting me in the center. That's why she's backed away. She figured things out pretty quickly." He turned toward me. "Yesterday morning, Will, when I saw how you are with her, I had to respect your place in her life."

"She's your daughter, Daniel," Luna said. "Will has not stood in the way of that, but it wouldn't have served Hannah for him to change the way he treats her. Can't you see that?"

"Luna, it's you I'm backing away from, not Hannah."

"You could back away from me and still do something with her. I could have handled that. You said you were coming here to see what you could do. Why don't you try something? Any little thing?"

"Luna, this trip began about us. You called me and left a message. I wrote. Our first calls were all about us. Pretty romantic stuff you threw at me. You touched that soft spot I guess I still have for you. I didn't tell you I was reluctant like I should have. Then I wasn't so reluctant anymore because you said very little about Hannah. I was still wary, but I figured our understanding hadn't changed. That I wasn't going to be involved as a father, like I said before Hannah was born. I'm not proud of that, but that's me."

"Threw at you?"

"That's how it felt. It worked."

"Are you done?"

"Almost. It's true I came to see what I could do, but only after you asked for that. And Hannah wasn't supposed to know I was her father. That's the agreement we made on the phone. Then on Saturday at the beach, you insisted we tell her. I was already feeling like I was letting myself get trapped. I should not have agreed. I felt guilty. It changed everything."

Luna shook her head back and forth and clenched her hands.

"Luna," I said. "That's a lot to answer. Will you?"

"Do I have to tell my version? It's not completely different from his, and I don't want to argue about details." She turned toward Daniel. "We messed it up. What matters is what you are going to do now."

Daniel looked back at me. "I wish we had some of whatever you've got."

"What does he have that you need?" Luna asked.

"It's what we need. Self-control. Discipline. Or maybe denial. I don't know. Something that keeps us at arms length until we can, I don't know, see things from a distance maybe. Something like that. We never built that in."

"How about an understanding of what a child needs?"

"I'm talking about being careful with each other. We never had that. I'd like to say you started it, but that doesn't make any difference, I suppose."

"But you can't give that care to your own child?" Luna resettled herself and shifted her gaze back and forth between us. "How much does this have to do with Will and me?'

"I already told you that has very little to do with, with the way I am."

"Very little is something."

"Listen to me. I believed you when you said nothing happened with Will. But when I was so late, couldn't you have trusted that I'd get here?"

"You didn't call to say you would be that late. I waited until two."

"Still, that's awfully quick. Going to Will."

"Well there it is. It has a lot to do with this."

"Look, Will is a man, and you can be so persuasive. I mean you got me here. I can deal with Friday night. I can believe that all you wanted from him was comfort. Besides I didn't see the sock until Saturday morning. By then you had me."

"Had you? Got you here?"

"Yes."

"If that's not it, what's the little part that does have to do with him?"

Daniel paused and took a breath, his glance going off into space. "When it comes to Hannah, he's a hard act to follow. It's hard enough for me to figure out what to do, but following that act? You gotta be kidding."

"You had a great example. You haven't thought to follow it. Will would step aside in a heartbeat. That's the kind of man he is. And yes, it was a mistake, asking him to bed."

Luna rose and went to the woodstove. She took the lid lifter from the mantel, removed the lid. Setting it aside, she peered into the dark interior.

"Will's got nothing to do with this," she went on. "He and Hannah and I have become something, and this is home now, but he is not her father or my man. So it comes down to what you will do with her. As for how I handled this, I can't take it back. But when you are right there in front of your child, it's still all excuses."

She put the lid back in place and turned to face him. "You've not tried a damn thing with her for two days. Why are you so afraid your whole being will dissolve when you touch her? Watching was never going to be enough."

"If I do something and it doesn't work, what then?"

"I haven't wanted to think about that." Luna looked at me, and only then did I notice her fighting tears, trying to draw them back. Her gaze travelled from one of us to the other. "Will, have you ever been swept away? I have, and I've let it take me over again, but with something good in mind, something important. The wrong way, but for something right. Daniel, I nested this place, Will's place, for you and me and Hannah. He gave that to me. I wanted to make this special so you could feel what a family could be like."

"I see that. I came into one."

"Would it have made a difference if that were not so?"

"I don't know. Now I have a question for you?"

"Sure."

"What would have happened if I had resisted your come-on when we started planning this? Would you have let me ease into being with Hannah my way?"

"My come-on?"

"Yes."

She leaned against the stove and touched its surface with her fingertips, letting them dance across it as if it were hot. Daniel put his elbows on his thighs and his head down. I thought I saw his body shuddering through his clothes. After a while, Luna returned to her place on the couch, taking up her crocheting from the basket at the base of the lamp, settling back, and looking for her place in the stitching.

"I won't give you more time than we planned for this visit. A week. We can say it's to see what happens, not what you can do. We can start counting now. But I won't wait like when I was pregnant, before there was a child wondering about a father. If a week isn't enough, go now."

"A week to make up my mind? I thought this could be a beginning of something, but we wouldn't know what that something is."

"Hannah needs some things certain in her life. As soon as possible."

"Is it a week to decide about Hannah or about Hannah and us?"

"It's a week."

Daniel looked up. "I want to say goodbye to her."

"Just like that? That's your answer?"

"We made a mistake, Luna."

"We made a child."

"I had to come do this."

"Do what, damn it? Do goddamned what? Stand around?"

"I want to say goodbye to her."

"It would be easier if I just made an excuse for you."

"She's asleep. At least while she's asleep."

"Suit yourself."

"You can make me into the bad guy."

"I'll stay away from that," she said, trembling. "If I could help her forget that she met her father, I would. That would hurt her less than to know you decided against her. But now she knows who you are. She won't forget. If she's lucky, it might not matter so much."

"You mean if...."

"I don't know what I mean."

Daniel sat there, still in his listener's pose, not moving.

"Go see her now. Then get your things and go."

"Couldn't we take some time to say goodbye? You and I?"

"It's too late for that, or too soon."

Luna set her things down and went back to the stove. Facing it, she leaned to the left and peered into the kindling box. "Not enough kindling to start a fire."

She picked up the box and hurried out. When she was gone, Daniel and I rose at the same moment and went toward each other, arms open. We embraced and held each other for what seemed the longest time. If he had been shaking before, there was no sign of it now. He felt almost light, as if a weight had lifted. When we unlocked, our hands went in unison to the crown of the other's head. Our foreheads touched. We tousled each other's hair like fathers do to their sons. I could not help but think that this was the outcome he had wanted all along.

He broke away. I did not turn to watch him leave through the hallway door, but I heard it click shut on more than one relationship that would never see another day. In the quiet I could hear the faint sound of Luna outside the woodshed, splitting kindling on the stump. From the rhythm of her sounds, I knew that she had never done it better. I wanted to see if her legs were spread wide enough and her blows going straight down through the wood like I had taught her. Thinking better of it, I turned away from the window, but there was a pause in the splitting. Unable to resist, I turned back.

She was retying her long mane, tucking it under her raincoat in a drizzle that had just begun. She was not done with her work, and the rain would not stop her. I knew she would remain out there until Daniel left through the front door. I went upstairs before she could see me watching.

WHEN I FIRST HEARD HER, it was past two, and I had been up reading for nearly an hour. During the year, dawn would be the time for me to notice Luna's sounds flavoring the quiet with unspoken meaning. The faucet turning on to fill a teapot, the teapot's simmer, cast iron clanking on a burner. A mother's voice answering a child's desire. The reassuring Luna sounds I had come to listen for. But at two in the morning under a mounting rain I did not hear the door from the back hallway open or Luna's feet padding across the hardwood toward the living room. Over the top of a newspaper I was thumbing through for stale news, I saw her coming toward me in her flannel pajamas. She settled into the far end of the couch. Tucking her legs under, hiding her small feet, so high-arched and pretty, she stretched her quilted robe over them, then reached beside her to turn on the wooden floor lamp she had placed there in anticipation of Daniel's visit. She looked at me with red, puffy eyes.

For the first time it occurred to me that Luna had a habit of showing, in a labored smile, her struggle for grim acceptance of painful things. Stoicism was difficult for her to gather, and it was far too soon for that. My eyes wandered about in their sockets while I tried to think of what to say. In a year I had not found a safe way to express care beyond the little things I had settled into doing to help Luna with Hannah and the game we played at finding names for what we shared. Yet that seemed enough to bind us together. Once again, it frightened me.

Lacking words, I returned Luna's tight expression but my face came loose in a grunt and a shake of my head. I might have even smiled.

"What was that about?" she asked.

"Self-deprecation."

"Not about...what you did today? What you did was just right."

"No. About not knowing what to say or do. Or even think."

"You've done more than enough."

"I don't like being tongue-tied when..."

"When what?"

"When you need attention. When I don't know what to do."

She looked away. "It rained like this on Friday night when we were up late. You had the house toasty then, too."

"One of us always does. You marveled at how the stove doesn't smoke with the lid off."

"I was distracting myself. Changing the subject."

"I thought so."

"I like to stare at the fire when things aren't going my way."

"What's that about?" I asked. "I'm not big on metaphor."

Luna smiled again, a bit less grim now, even amused. "It keeps me warm when I'm feeling cold, and it lights my way. A lawyer might not appreciate symbols, but a blacksmith would, especially about fire."

"In the old days, villages sometimes imprisoned blacksmiths in their forges to keep them from leaving. They were indispensable. I don't think the emphasis was on symbols."

"Isn't there some romance in rekindling the old ways?"

"Those ways seem more satisfying and independent in a complicated world, that's all. Like wood heat. Buying cords from a local or cutting your own. Splitting and stacking, keeping it dry, tending the fire. That or flip a switch, hear a fan, pay a power company. I'd get off the power grid if I could."

"No romance in that at all?"

I smiled. "Nope. Not a bit."

"When you taught me about this stove and showed me how to keep it from smoking when the lid is off, you glowed like the fire. When you showed me striking at the anvil, you called it a dance. You told Daniel that welding with only your fire and hammer is magic."

"I get carried away sometimes."

"I rest my case."

I rose and went to the woodstove, standing close enough to feel its heat on the front of my legs.

"You must be real sad," I said.

"Not like I expected. No more millstone around my neck."

"You feel free?"

"From something, which is enough for now. And I'm not alone. I have a friend."

"How 'bout I crank this up and add a log?"

She nearly grinned. "We hardly need it. Would you like some tea?"

"Sure."

Luna unpacked herself from her coziness and rose to her feet. She tightened her quilted robe, stretched herself from raised toes to leaned-back head, then walked to the kitchen with a little two-step that surprised me. I surmised that something she had to do was finished now, and she was moving on. Leaning on the far counter, she reached toward the cabinets, rummaged through tea boxes until she found the one she wanted, leaned to her left on one leg and found our cups - mine with the family of wolves, hers the elephants. I loved watching her fullness press into whatever she was wearing. She filled the teapot and lit a burner. Done, she rounded the counter and perched on the stool closest to the woodstove just as I closed the lid and shut down the jets on either side for a less ravenous burn. I turned.

"I'm not sure you needed me for this."

"There's your self-deprecation. You were just right. Not too much, not too little. Just like with Hannah."

I swallowed.

"I'm sad and angry and full of self-blame for something I doubt could ever have come right."

"So matter-of-fact for you."

"A mask, at least for tonight. Acting's the best place to start believing."

"Seems I've heard that from you before." I opened the stove lid. Inside, the smoke curled around the burning logs, then vanished in the broad blast of air. "What went wrong," I asked, "that got you wanting my help?"

"Daniel's version wasn't too far off. I started off on the wrong foot and never got it right, never looked back until it was too late. I could see Daniel hiding panic. I could feel him withdraw. Then I got angry and behaved badly. He just took it. That's when I thought of you. Maybe I used you to get us to the end in a better way, and you did, really. But I wasn't thinking of that. I don't think I had given up."

She took a deep breath. "I wish I could have done this without your help. Without you having to worry about me."

"It was okay." I replaced the stove lid. "I'm a big boy."

Luna looked right at me. "Without many friends. If you met Daniel on his own terms, you could have been good friends. He would have been good for you."

"How so?"

"He is a passionate free spirit. You withhold yourself."

"It takes one to know one."

"I haven't always been this way."

"Nor have I."

The teapot approached a whistle. She turned and stretched across the counter to shut down the burner, twisting onto her stomach to reach it. Her feet came out straight behind her, right in front of me. I reached out and cradled one in my hands.

She didn't jump up in surprise or pull away, but turned without alarm, leaving her foot in my hands. When I let go, she slid back down to the stool and tucked her feet out of sight beneath her robe.

"Seems like two people don't often reach the same point at the same time," she said. "And if they do, it's often not by a good path. Has it been that way for you?"

"Always."

"You're the matter-of-fact one, but then you do something like this." She let one foot peek out and beamed the warmest smile. "Or let a dream slip out." She raised herself to the counter and scooted back to pour the tea.

I turned around, found the lid lifter on the mantel, and began to open the stove. Then Luna was beside me, placing her hand on top of mine.

"Please don't open it again."

"Too warm?"

"You're trying to escape, just like me."

I needed only a quarter turn to face her and find myself so close I could feel the breath from her nose on my cheeks. We clasped our hands, laced our fingers, held them between us in a tightening knot.

"Luna," I began, "this isn't a good time for us to change anything. I want to make love with you, but that's all I know for sure about what I want. That's a bum deal for you and Hannah. A very bum deal. And I'd do it."

"Tonight I want to be next to you. I don't want to be alone, good as that might be for me."

"My room," I said. "You'll like it. We'll keep all the doors open to hear Hannah."

We dropped our hands. She followed me up the stairs.

I CURLED AROUND HER, weaving my fingers into hers, pulling her to me. When we were still, it occurred to me that my experience with intimate love had been too much about passion. Giving warmth and care for a soul in need without speeding past them was mostly new. And accompanied by fear. I thought maybe I could do it, but I wasn't sure. Then Luna spoke.

"Friday night I said there's a story you haven't told me."

"Sounds like a request, pardner."

"Pardner," she answered. "That's a name we didn't think of."

"Probably not a good one. I guess I should tell you a story."

"Not now, but someday soon. I have another thought."

"What's that?" I asked.

"You haven't had this, or it turned bad."

"Rarely got through the passion, and when I did, I never learned what to do next."

"Me, too, though I've tried."

We stayed curled and awake for the longest time, with little said. There was only the sound of frogs until the rain began in a pounding wind that I thought might bring down a few shallow-rooted pines behind the shop. Soon it tempered, became intermittent, indecisive, then stopped altogether. Random drops splashed off the trees whenever a hint of wind returned.

"Was that thunder?" I asked. "In a Northcoast rain?"

"Yes," Luna answered. "Maybe some lightning will happen."

"Is that a car I hear coming? Not many come this late."

Luna mumbled a laugh. "No need to worry. He won't come back. Let's try not to think about him."

The ducks hardly squawked, and I couldn't hear them splashing in the puddles. When the branches no longer scraped the window, I whispered that the rain had really stopped.

"We've had enough," Luna said, sliding away but not far. She arranged herself on her back, arching herself for a few seconds in the way I like, only better because she was prone. I wanted to reach for her, but she was breathing with such intention. I thought it best to leave her alone. She was working hard to let go.

"Your room is so cozy and warm above the wood stove," she said. "But with the big windows on either side, it feels like being outside."

"Inside and out at the same time," I answered.

"Real nice."

"Maybe you'll come again soon."

"Maybe."

We drifted away. Once, I awakened hot and found her wrapped around me, fast asleep but holding on. One of us had kicked off a blanket, an adjustment to having two bodies heating a space that had been used by only one. I moved away to cool down.

Just after sunrise, I had to pee and found myself alone in my bed. A sound drew me downstairs. In my drowsiness, I thought it was a door closing. A note waited for me on the counter. I read it as another door shut at the back of the house. The note said only this:

Will,

I left at first light. I had to. Best way to keep a promise to myself. I am going to sleep until Hannah gets me up. She's deep into it, still escaping, and I need to as well. So it won't be soon. Nothing should be soon, or maybe not at all. Please help me with that.

I still have no name for us and hope you don't either. Let's not try to find the word. Let's find the thing first. Then naming it will be easy.

Luna

I wrote my name under hers, then showered and hurried off for work before she could awaken. Wanting the day to feel like any other, I planned on stopping for my customary morning breakfast. I would sit near the broad windows of

Los Bagels, enjoy the morning sun, my sesame bagel with cream chees, walnuts and raisins, and the paper. I would say hello to people I know and wonder what it would be like when I got home.

BROTHERHOOD IN BEIJING

AFTER WHAT SEEMS LIKE a random dozen turns, I point to the Beijing map in my lap and plead with my cabbie, "Temple Of Heaven?" He grins, taps his forehead with his forefinger, zigzags through another tangle of cars and cabs, trucks and buses, bikes and motorcycles, scooters and pedestrians. I fold the map along its torn creases, nod, return it to my shirt pocket, and give in to his lefts and rights to nowhere.

Twice more I pull out my map and open it. Twice more he smiles and taps his head. Negotiating the next labyrinthine intersection, he eases the map from my hands, folds, returns it to my pocket. I offer an uncertain smile as he dots and darts through the moving maze. When we pass Tiananmen Square, I am certain we are taking the longest way.

A minute later the bright, tiled domes of the temple materialize, and my cabbie grins again. In a few blocks he swerves through the commotion, finds the curb, stops on a dime, and pokes a button on his state-of-the art dashboard. A ticket clicks out of a slot in the middle. I reach into my pocket and fumble with the different denominations of green, pink, orange and blue bills with the pictures of Mao beaming down from the upper left corner. My cabbie pulls three of different colors from my hands.

"That all," he says. Then, tapping his head once more and smiling his biggest smile, he raises his arm, bent at the elbow. I do the same. Lacing our arms together and grasping hands, we lean in and press our foreheads together.

A horn toots behind us. We pull apart.

"China," he says.

THE BLUE NOTE

FROM THE DOORWAY Kate Squires watches her husband. He is standing at the desk in the windowless back corner of the living room, keys in hand. In the glow of his chestnut lamp, which she tolerates because he loves it so, Kal peers down at their mammoth dictionary, the one Ms. Shelby, the iconic old librarian at her school, insisted every teacher buy. The one he has come to love when the spirit of a word search comes over him. He looks good, she thinks, in his dark woolen overcoat with his plaid scarf tucked in. She has always liked the scarf's blacks and grays that match his turning hair. She likes his long, straight nose pointing past his broad chin and the way his long fingers graze the pages in the same way they run out a pleasant rhythm on their piano. How long ago was it, she wonders, that she loved that nose nuzzling her, those hands touching her. Early this morning, when she approached him in bed and he again succumbed to her advances, she found herself thinking she might love them again, for in the long weeks since she told him, he has begun to treat their relationship like a delicate vase brought down from atop a high, undusted shelf. She swallows the bittersweet taste of watching him work toward something she is not sure of, yet rising within her is a silent prayer that it will continue.

Kate watches Kal study the page. In the last few years, the delight he takes in being surprised by a relationship between certain words has remained one of the endearing qualities she finds in him. The last time she saw him standing over the open dictionary, those fingers suspending the corner of a page, was during that first week after she told him. From a note he had scribbled and left on the desk, so unlike his orderly ways, she knew what words he had been pondering. Manual and manipulate. Later that day, when she asked about them, he told her they grew from the Latin word for hand. She hid her embarrassment that she, the English teacher, had not seen it.

"I wonder if "manna" is connected," he said.

"A blessing from heaven," she answered.

"Maybe someday we'll see all this as a blessing," he said under his breath.

"You should still be mad," she answered. All that week she had been waiting for torrents of anger, but after the first day no more came. It still astonishes her.

"How can I be, with all the love-making?" he had said. She was glad he used that word. "Shipping Jake and Addie off to the Sorensons' so we can have nights alone. Anything I want, every night. I go to work exhausted."

"I ship the kids off for their sake, too, you know. They don't need so much time around this."

As she watches him in the soft light, she thinks about her seduction the day she told him. The kids already at the neighbors, her candlelight dinner and their most expensive bottle of wine, the dried-out marijuana she found buried in the back of their filing cabinet. Their bodies, superheated with tension, making the sex so frenzied and good. She remembers him shivering under the touch of her fingers, succumbing to her advances. She never asked. He never resisted. When they were done, they turned away and slept on opposite sides of the bed, like always.

That the dictionary is open again is a good sign, she thinks, but his timing concerns her. What could be on his mind but this meeting tonight with his discarded buddy? With great reluctance he had accepted David's request for what Kal was calling "David's Necessary Acknowledgment." Whatever it will be, she thinks, putting themselves through it makes no sense, makes her want to protect both of them by saying no, don't, but she has no standing to intervene.

She bites her lip and wonders how tough on David he will be and what combination of words he might be contemplating deeply enough to make him late. If he is to be at The Blue Note at five, half an hour away, he needs to leave now. Kal is never late.

He looks up, but not at her and stares at the flickering bulb inside the lamp's beat-up old shade. It backlights his profile. I love that, she thinks, but will I get back to loving him? And he to me? She imagines David waiting at the bar, watching for Kal through the long glass ovals of The Blue Note's doors. On how many afternoons had David waited with practiced patience in his car until she drove by the entrance to Redwood Park and stopped around the corner? At their meeting place in the big trees, on their walk back to his car or hers, they never touched, but on the way to the motel David's calm veneer always dissolved into an urgency that disturbed her. Though propelled by the same haste, sometimes she wanted to set it aside so that their destination and result would not always be the same. She gave in every time.

She thinks about how much less she misses David now but accepts she hasn't succeeded in draining herself of him. The thought brings back a picture. A motel picture. It blunts the enthusiasm she has been trying to bring to the project of healing. Project, she wonders. Is that what this is?

She sees Kal in her car in the parking lot behind his office the day she told him. A Friday like this one at about the same time, their customary hour for drinks in their corner booth at The Blue Note. She cringes at the memory of letting it slip out that she and David had stopped at The Blue Note for coffee that night, of Kal screaming that they go there right away. Telling him that was a huge mistake she later thought might be self-punishment.

Going home that night to the seduction she had planned, she expected him, the domestic lawyer who thrived on custody battles, to negate her plan, swallow his anger, and head straight for a course of action that would keep their family together or cleave it into workable halves. When instead he fell into grasping for angles of insight, for swimming, he said, in the puddle of his feelings, she figured she could make the evening work, and that it would be a good start toward...toward what? Something she was so unsure of. Even more surprising, he followed that night with defaulting into numbed silence. Only after the first week did he rediscover his lawyer's mind and begin interrogating her about the first time with David. Even then his examination lacked that first anger, came from behind a wall, didn't last long. His silence returned and by degrees became the thoughtfulness of timid favors. Flowers one night; taking off an afternoon from another; a fine family dinner that took most of a Saturday to prepare, its presentation filled with awkward quiet. What a rollercoaster ride those first weeks were, but she tried to be heartened. Now, watching him resume his old dictionary habit with such seriousness at a time like this, she thinks it might not be so good. She worries that what he might learn tonight will throw them into reverse.

She starts toward him from the archway between the living room and the front hall. "What are your words this time?" When he shuts the dictionary and turns toward her, she stops and returns her hand to the frame of the archway.

"Nothing that would interest you." His face mirrors the tightness she feels in hers. "I should go now," he says.

"Sort of a funny time to be distracted by a little word match." Immediately she regrets her words and timing.

He fixes a frown at her. "This one's not little."

"I didn't mean to diminish it. Just feeling insecure."

"Who has more to worry about?"

"There's no more David," she says, a hint of fatigue in her voice.

"When does trust return?" he asks, his voice nearly a whisper.

She sighs. "I still don't know what to say when you ask that." When he comes to her, she risks a hand on his shoulder. "This is new to us."

He doesn't move away from her. "Are there other things you haven't told me?"

"Please let's not."

"I'm going to sit him in our booth and make him suffer."

For two months now she had tried to believe that he was choosing David for the bigger share of his anger because David was an easier target. There wasn't as much for him to lose, a growing friendship sure enough, but wouldn't that be easy to discard after such an insult?

Besides, his anger, save for the very beginning, was so much less than she expected. She wonders if she has she been wrong to soften him with so much lovemaking. It has been so good, as if sex borne of guilt burns with such extraordinary tension and release. But was it right? Didn't it obscure what they needed?

She wonders why Kal has insisted on The Blue Note to inflict what he has been calling deserved damage. She flashes back to that moment in his office parking lot when he screamed that they must go immediately to the place she had soiled, how she begged him not to, how she had already arranged for Jake and Addie to be gone, and all that passionate sex. Weeks later, she remembers, he admitted to a confusing polarity in the way he responded to the two who had done this to him.

"You know he has agreed to meet me at The Blue Note?" he had asked her.

"Yes, Kal. You told me."

"In our place that you took from us," he says.

"Punish me," she answers. "What do you gain by punishing him?"

"I'll let you know after I do it."

Tonight she knows she should not challenge what he is doing, but she can't let go of a question. She removes her hand from his shoulder.

"Mind if I ask what's in this for you? I mean, what are you really going to get from it?"

He presses his lips together in a tight line and shakes his head. "Please don't ask again. I said I don't know. I don't even know what I'm going to say."

She leans forward and wanders a kiss in the general direction of his mouth, hoping his lips would meet hers halfway. They do, with the barest of touching.

At the door the cold pours in on a March wind. "See you later," he says. For these two months he has been saying that in the same uncertain voice almost every time either of them leaves the house. She thinks that maybe his need for this so-called acknowledgement is the way he can close the books on David without closing them on her. And that she has got to match that. Yes, she decides, that is what it's all about.

She hears the rumble of Kal's old Mercedes, a sound she still loves. She sees David hovering on the edges of her mind. At school he had kept doing things to keep himself there until, in the privacy of her classroom during a prep period, she whispered a scream for him to stay away. After that, a hand grazing her shoulder in the copying room that sent shivers down her spine. A card in her mailbox in the teachers' room that spoiled a prep period. A flower under the windshield wiper that brought tears. A note dropped through the crack at the top of her car window almost got her to the motel one more time. He was so careless. It took being cold and staying angry to get him to back away.

Still she can taste him.

At the window Kate watches Kal backing the Mercedes down the driveway. She imagines herself standing under the milky glow of a street lamp, looking into The Blue Note from across the glistening pavement, watching Kal and David through an oval window under the arcs of neon tubes that spell "The Blue Note" along the top of each one. She sees their stiff strides from the mahogany bar to that damaged booth where she knows Kal will take him, their blue faces staring into the rain. She thinks of Kal's favorite song, "I Think It's Gonna Work Out Fine," one of the few that could still get him onto The Blue Note's dance floor after the glow of the early years wore away. She remembers how their favorite date had long ago become a perfunctory ritual, his song a platitude he hummed and hid behind when she tried to tell him they were becoming ships passing in the night. Those memories, already diminished by the distance that had grown, she has now spoiled forever. She thinks he must be trying to rub out all those walks and hikes, those dinners and movies with David and Joellen and the kids, all their baseball and soccer games, everything that had sprung from the way their families came together through work and school, all that growing closeness looping in and out of her secret with David, quilting together so much good and so many lies.

She has half a mind to wait a few minutes and follow. A show of commitment would help Kal close out this difficult time and hasten the passage for David. And for herself through the new unknowns. Or she could settle for watching them from across the street, in the rain, through The Blue Note's neon-lit windows. Or she could start a fire, set the candles, and dress again in the way she was certain would draw him close.

IT IS ONE OF THOSE AGGRAVATING FOGS that require additional wiper speeds between the only two his old Mercedes has. Kal slows, watches for taillights, checks for landmarks on 101 between Arcata and Eureka. He wonders what happened to the clear, chosen destinations he and Kate have without intention replaced with looking back on the way things have not worked out. Why had he never thought about preparing for the unexpected? It seemed to happen to almost every client. He had made his living from their neglects and bad surprises but never thought one would happen to him.

He remembers their two families walking on the wet sand of Moonstone Beach on a Saturday morning, the four kids skittering like shore birds along the edge of the tiny surf. He sees Joellen walking beside him, Kate and David in front, widening the gap, turning toward each other, swinging their hands close, almost touching. And Joellen distracting him with occasional bumps of shoulders, her voice too eager, her timing too obvious as if she was trying to compete rather than deal with it. He remembers the flutter in his heart the first time he returned her deliberate bumps of arms and hips, her playful gab, so close to invitation. The frightening thrill of unacceptable possibility. He sees them slowing down, widening the gap even further, their fingers brushing a few times, but himself hardly looking at her. He could not take his eyes off Kate and David.

The scene disappears and another comes, a Friday night dinner at home with both families. Like always, Kate and David got there first, Joellen last. Passing by the kitchen window, he sees them leaning toward each other by the counter, chatting and laughing, sipping wine, only a few feet separating them. Each has a hand on the counter, which seems like a brake they use to resist falling into each other. He sees the bottle of wine standing half-empty and how they place their glasses close to it as if to keep drinking before he joins them would amount to exclusion. He sees that there is no third glass. When he enters, Kate edges away from David. They quiz him about his day, but still there is no third glass, no offer to pour him one. He recalls how distant she seemed, how mechanical their questions, how unwelcome he felt, and that he did not go to kiss her, instead grabbing a beer from the refrigerator and joining the kids in staring at the television in the family room until Joellen arrived.

He thinks of an even bigger hint of trouble. At a party at the Korbels' a few months before Kate told him, David showed slides of the camping trip they had taken that summer with the kids to a lake in the Sierras. The slides favored Kate in number. Those featuring her were clear and well-arranged, with faded backgrounds that isolated her profile or showed the side of her breast at the edge of her tank top or her swimming suit cutting high across her butt, as if he were trying to give Kate and himself away. Those featuring Joellen, him and the kids were ordinary and cluttered. Where everyone was present in a single slide, Kate seemed apart in sharper focus.

In front of the screen Kate and David sat on the couch, their hands stretching vaguely toward each other's. It was the moment that finally ratcheted up the worry he was so good at excusing away. He moved to the back of the couch and watched David's left hand move back and forth from projector to couch, each time a little closer to Kate's fingers. From the side he could see her face expressionless as she looked unfailingly straight ahead. Only when David's fingertips had advanced to within an inch or two did she pull hers back, and then not far. He remembers what he said when he bent to her ear.

"I want to go home," he whispered.

"Can we wait a few minutes?" she asked, her voice quivering. She turned her face upward and held his gaze. "Five minutes, I promise. Jake and Addie are staying here."

"I know. I packed their stuff."

She kept her promise. He bounced the car down the Korbels' bumpy gravel road.

"Please slow down," she said.

"We're almost to the pavement."

"You okay?"

"Is there anything I should know?"

"No," she said her voice just above a whisper. Her eyes turned toward his, but he kept his gaze on the road.

"I shouldn't worry?"

Kate's eyes flitted about for a moment, found his again, rested there. "No, you shouldn't."

Now, driving through the dense fog, Kal thinks that difficult night should have trapped him in a funk, but he remembers how his mind plays tricks on itself, his body administers a fear-killing drug when he doesn't want to face something. Even then he did not give up the illusion that Kate and David were early in a benign story, their flirting little more than both couples had been playing at on the beach. He remained convinced that they would go no further. Now he wonders if having awakened then would have made a difference.

The fog thins but he keeps his speed at a pace to suit his wondering. He thinks of when he met Joellen in that custody matter a year before. He hears her strong voice on the phone and sees her self-assurance in the courtroom when she testified for his client. There were the calls he had made before the hearing to confirm details of the custody report she had already sent and knew he had received. There were her return calls to confirm what she had confirmed before. And how he began to notice her in the courthouse. The way glanced at each other in the hallways and chatted with strained politeness. He began to understand, for the first time, how lonely he was in marriage. He recalls deciding to push Joellen aside and his feeling that she did the same, but how their families' growing friendship renewed their careful stares and the little games they began to play.

The windshield wipers squeak against the glass. What would have happened had he and Joellen worked together every day like Kate and David? "It doesn't matter," he says aloud. He tries to think only about getting through this meeting. How strange it is, he says inside, to forgive my wife but not my great new friend. How can I face him, he thinks, without trying for some measure of forgiveness, however small? Forgetting wasn't going to happen.

David's car sits in front of The Blue Note. Kal passes it and parks in the next block. On the sidewalk he watches the fog swirl in the milky light of the street lamps and wonders again why this angry tide washes only toward David. Nor does it seem to matter that the difference between making and not making the same mistake might have been as little as a few more not-so-accidental touches, a few encouraging words in the courthouse halls. He is sure Kate and David began that way.

As he shuts off the engine he sighs, wonders which motel they used, wishes against his best judgment that he could have been behind the wall, seeing through it, watching.

WHEN THE SOUND OF KAL'S CAR fades, Kate goes to the dictionary. She remembers that a few times when she had pushed open a book she had just closed, it returned to the same place as if the pages and the crease in the binding have something like memory. Pushing at the edge, taking care to withdraw her fingers quickly, she arrives at pages 476 and 477. "Foreteller to formula." She scans the first column. "Forget. To cease or omit to think about something." I'd like to think it's a meaningful coincidence, she says to herself, but Kal could have been right on this page, trying like she is to decide if forgetting is possible. Not so, but the years might take away the colors, leaving only transparencies that have lost their power. They could hope for that.

She leaves the dictionary open and wanders to the middle of the room. Sitting down on the rug, she stares into the empty fireplace.

During the prep period she shared with David two falls ago, her first year at Eureka High, they tiptoed around their attraction, talking about their spouses with measured fondness, delighting in learning of the two couples' shared interests: each had a child starting at the middle school, each a third grader beginning Tee Ball; they liked foreign and independent movies, the Wabash Diner in Eureka, the bagel deli after Saturday morning walks, illegal fireworks at Moonstone Beach on the Fourth of July, backpacking, The Blue Note. Kate, the new teacher, sought his advice. David, the veteran, went out of his way to help. In the mornings he smelled fresh, with a hint of a menthol she was surprised to like. They made a habit of waiting in line together for the copier and chatted exclusively in spite of the stares. At faculty meetings they sat in the back, lightening the interminable hour with doodling, competing to find new words in the letters of a vowel-filled word written at the top of a blank sheet of paper. Their legs bumped under the table, their fingers touched during the exchange of the pen. By November they were taking lunch and prep period in his room or hers. They would face each other in student desks, joking and laughing about the kids they shared.

She thinks of the statement she made to him one day when they were watching the lunch crowd enter the cafeteria. "I think you sell kids short, David." She felt bold telling him that. She hadn't earned the right to question a seasoned pro.

There were teachers all around. She kept her voice down and tried not to look at him.

He said only "It will happen to you," singing it like the love song, but almost a whisper. When his eyes surveyed her, Kate shifted her gaze toward the row of windows.

"I suppose that things you hope won't happen often do," she said.

"Some things are inevitable."

"Why are you staring at me?"

"Just thinking," David answered. "About what you said."

"Am I too judgmental for a beginner?"

"No. I meant your remark about things you hope won't happen. I want to ask you something."

Kate tried to keep her gaze on the windows. "What?"

"Maybe we should meet each other's mates."

She felt relieved and disappointed. "You've sort of met at the kids' games, and at school. But yes, introductions, plans, that sort of thing."

"We should do that."

"Yes, we should," she said. "But let's stop talking now."

Unsettled by the memory of her urgency, she rises and goes back to the dictionary, but the memories follow her. The day it began, a Friday. Kal in Seattle on a big case, Joellen with her kids at her mother's in Portland. She saw it coming. The cocktail of longing, fear, guilt and excitement roiling in her gut hadn't prevented her from lingering in her classroom at the end of the day, tidying up beyond need, bouncing between hoping David would and would not appear at her door. Just as she was putting on her coat, he did. He stayed in the doorway. They stared.

"Let's have dinner," he said.

Her eyes meet his. "Not dinner. After, for dessert. I'll get them to my mother's."

She remembers the disgust she felt at that impersonal reference to her children, at the certainty she felt about the night set out before her. She sees again the reflection of her face in the car window as she fumbled unlocking the door. She sees the tears and bitten lip in the rearview mirror as she watched David take his exit off the freeway. It had not felt like love beginning.

In the light of Kal's lamp, she searches the next column. "Forgive. To grant free pardon for an offense or debt."

"He won't do that tonight with David," she says aloud. He's a lawyer preparing for a hearing with his wife's ex-lover, planning his cross-examination. He would pound David with his words.

She thinks about following him. She could soften it for them.

Swallowing, she closes the dictionary and walks to the front window. Often David had irked her with his unwillingness to confront reality, but she wasn't much better. Once after making love, he stood in front of curtains closed to traffic passing the motel. He was buttoning his shirt and staring at her with that engrossed smile that was becoming too much for her. But with her hunger still alive, her skin and flesh wanting more of his fingers and lips skimming and pulling, she had risen from the bed and gone to him, her hands following his up his shirt, unbuttoning as he buttoned. She pulled him toward the bed, violating the ticking clock, and he followed.

"This is perfect," he said, letting her pull him down over her. "I don't want to lose it."

"This is anything but perfect," she answered.

His hands glided over her, barely touching. She loved his light touch right through her growing irritation.

"Are you ready to give this up?" he asked.

"I don't know. Not yet. Don't talk."

"Don't say not yet." He pulled her up to him.

"Not yet," she said again. She remembers the authority in her voice. That was their last time.

A gust of wind splatters drops of water from the cypress branches against the window. Her nose bumps the chilly pane. Closing her eyes she sees her two men sitting across from each other in the booth, Kal questioning, David struggling to answer. They are under the stone arches and pastel plaster walls curving into the ceiling, suffused by blue diner neon. In the early years, the good ones, Kal and she sat in their corner booth and watched the hawking singles crowd. Sometimes they pretended to be part of the scene, overplaying The Blue Note like new lovers, letting hard liquor loosen them into flirting and kissing across the table. She would move to Kal's side of the booth. Laughing at themselves and leaning on each other, they would settle into guessing who had not yet slept with whom but would that night for the first time.

"How shallow that seems, now," she whispers. From the long distance of their disappointing years, she now finds that time so very insufficient, so avoidant.

She thinks of a boyfriend she had dumped in high school. At their tenth reunion, after a few friendly words, he handed her a pack of matches. On the tucked-in cover side, bright cursive letters announced that "It Don't Hurt Anymore." She figures that might be the most they should expect for a while, maybe longer.

Perhaps someday they could go to The Blue Note again. Just the two of them.

THROUGH THE OVAL WINDOWS in The Blue Note's doors, Kal sees David leaning against the bar. David turns and straightens, his elbows searching behind him for a purchase on the bar's surface. Finding it too high, they hang there, lost. He folds his hands at his waist.

Kal stands by the empty stool to David's right. "Let's take a booth and have a beer." He surveys the window booths as if he were making a choice and starts for the one he has already chosen. The waitress arrives as soon as they are settled.

"Hi Dana. I'll have a Beck's draft," Kal says before she can speak, avoiding their customary chitchat.

She says hello and smiles through her small, full lips. A small mouth like Kate's, just as pretty.

"And you?" she asks David.

"The same, thanks," he answers, his voice quiet and breathy.

"Sure." She turns and hurries off.

"She's got a mouth like Kate's, don't you think?" Kal asks.

David holds up his hands, palms facing out. "I know you're going to cross-examine me, but please, not that."

"I figure I'm entitled."

David nods. "I was hoping to avoid it with a huge apology."

"Don't even try." Kal stares. "You and Kate came here after the first time, didn't you?"

"We did that."

"It was a Friday night?"

David nods again, his lips drawn down in a deep frown.

"Our place on a Friday night."

"I don't know what to say."

"Try yes. Remember when the four of us had dinner here?"

"Yes."

"What night was that?"

"A Friday."

"Right. Kate tried to get us to go somewhere else. Remember?"

David takes a deep breath. "Are only yes and no answers permitted?"

"I thought she was trying to protect our spot, but you guys were doing it then, right?"

"Right."

"I'm still pissed at her for coming here with you. The little things still piss me off."

"That's what Joellen says. Kate didn't choose this place that night. I did."

"Don't protect her. You wandered in here from wherever you did it without giving it much of a thought."

"We did, but it..."

"Stop right there. You're not going to tell me this place was too convenient?"

"Do I have to answer that?"

"Forget about it. You couldn't possibly score any points."

David shrugged. "I hope I can score a few, somehow."

"Forget about that, too." He paused and put both hands on the table. "Kate and I have good reasons to stay together. Give me some reasons to stay your friend."

He notices Dana rounding the corner of the bar. He thinks to ask David how he liked kissing perky little mouths like hers, like Kate's, but David is too erect and stiff, his hands folded on the table, his lips remaining in a grim line. Too easy a target for shots like that.

"Your beers, gentlemen," Dana says, making just the quickest eye contact as she sets their glasses before them. "Should I run a tab?"

"No thanks," Kal says. "One will be enough. Could you do the tabs separately?"

"I can do that," Dana answers as she turns without asking what else they might want.

"David, what would you say is the biggest problem I have with you?"

"Forgetting?"

"Forgetting is out of the question. Try again."

"Forgiving?"

Kal withholds a sneer. "You got it. What do you think makes forgiving so hard?"

"You're too good at this, and I've a lousy case."

"You have no case. Just answer the question."

"Because I deceived you. Kal, I want to listen to how you feel and then apologize."

"You'll get more points for a wrong answer than a worthless apology."

"I'm not going to get any points."

"You're right, but you owe me. Make another guess. What makes forgiving so hard?"

"That we became friends during this."

"Exactly. How could you do such a shitty thing to a friend?"

"You're not going to believe me."

"Try me."

"Joellen and I had been without good friends for so long. And she really likes Kate. I wanted to keep that for us for as long as I could."

"What about great sex and the feeling of being loved? You wanted to keep that, too, didn't you?"

"That, too."

"That mostly." Kal looks out into the darkness, then back. "Love, huh?"

David shifts and pushes his hands against the seat. "This is like confession where the priest is the victim."

"And I'm a priest who thought about getting into your wife's pants. She thought about mine, too."

David tries a half-smile. "Joellen talks about that."

"We liked each other when we met in the courthouse, starting with that case. A lot. We flirted in the hallways. We stopped. Then watching you and Kate, we got like mockingbirds. This story could have been different."

"I hope that gets me a little understanding."

"Not a shred. There's a big difference. We resisted. You didn't."

Their eyes meet and hold for what seems an interminable moment.

"You started it, right?" he asks.

"Is that what Kate said?"

"Sort of. She won't say much."

"She's partly right."

"I can see it. I can't not see it. At some point you both knew it was coming, and you quit trying to stop it. You took the first chance, I'm sure of that. She stopped you without conviction, so you waited a few minutes and tried again with better results. But what the hell. It started way before that."

David leans forward and puts his elbows on the table. "That's no excuse."

"A bit late to say, don't you think? That's as close as I'll let you get to an apology."

"At least I got it in. Maybe later you'll take more."

"I doubt it. Are you and Joellen going to make it?"

"We've been trying for the kids, but it's a pretense. I'll be moving out soon. Eventually away."

"The farther away you go the better. Kate thinks you can stay friends, and I'm not supposed to feel threatened. I don't think you can cut out intimacy and expect friendship to survive, but I'm going to respect her need. When will you leave?"

"I hope this summer so the kids can visit me right away."

"Where?"

"Wherever in this state I can teach. How do we get to the end of this?"

Kal rises and puts his hands in his pockets. "You've had enough. Let's finish this way. Don't ask me to trust or forgive. If either happens you'll be the second to know. Don't expect me to forget, and don't 'fuck with my marriage."

David nods and rises to his feet. "You're letting me off easy. Maybe someday we could try to be friends again."

"In another lifetime. This meeting has been good for me, but not that good."

"I'll pick up the tabs."

"No, this one's on me."

KATE GETS HER COAT from the closet, turns on the porch light, and opens the door to a clearing sky. She sees herself walking arm-in-arm down Third Street with David after four hours in a South Broadway motel, the bloom of something new, love or whatever, not strong enough to smother guilt. After, they were through the doors of The Blue Note before she could gather her wits enough to say no. She realizes that it was as automatic for her as it was for him, as if the inevitability had meaning. Or that, the damage done, it didn't matter. She laughs at the memory of the promise she made to herself that night. Not to go there with David again, the easy promise to make.

Motels became weekday fare after school on the days Kal picked up the kids, and there were the occasional weekend afternoons. Alone, she never called what they did love, but to David she did, at first. It felt good. "I love you" when she not so gently bit his lip and turned him over to keep the smell of motel cigarettes from her hair, when she felt his tongue raise her nipples and trace a slow line down her stomach. In the haste of those escapes, sex took them over and left time for little else. The secrecy and lies made each time guilt-ridden, fearful, but delicious. Obscenely delicious, leaving her staring at her reflection in a cracked bathroom mirror, then hurrying home after five o'clock to a quick bath, lots of shampoo, and Kal's wondering glances over warmed-over dinner with grouchy kids.

Hunching over the wheel, she creeps her car through pockets of fog in the dips, squinting toward the road while the defroster works in millimeters to clear the windshield. When the car warms, she slouches back into the seat and stares over the broken line of treetops. She watches silver-topped clouds scud by, the moon moving in and out, racing somewhere, like she wanted to.

She relives how she told Kal without overture, blurting it out in the car parked behind the old Victorian that housed his office on Second Street. The words stick in her mind as if they had been carved.

"Kal, David and I are lovers. Since you went to Seattle last October. We've been living a huge lie right in front of you, but it's over now. I'm not going to do it anymore. I'm..."

"Stop!" he screamed. His eyes were huge. He slumped and stared and his mouth dropped open. He turned away.

"Say something," Kate said. "Tell me what you feel and what you're going to do."

He drew himself up straight. "You're telling me this in a panic. You're afraid of something else. What's going on?"

"Joellen figured it out today. I was afraid she would get to you first."

"You've been fucking him and only tell me after you got caught, and I'm supposed to believe it's over? How long have you been fucking him, Kate? Where do you fuck him? Jesus, Kate, do you love him? Did you fuck him in our bed when I was in Seattle? When...."

"Stop! Please! No, never in our bed. I should have told you sooner, but I wasn't ready to stop. I know how bad that sounds. I've stopped now."

"When was the last time?"

"Please, no. It won't help to know."

"What's it like with him? I want to know what it's like!"

"No you don't. It won't help."

"I should have stopped trusting you a long time ago. So many signs. When I asked, you said not to worry. I should have trusted my instincts. I should have fucked Joellen. I could have, but I didn't. I should have..."

"Please stop! Let's go home."

"I can't fake it in front of the Jake and Addie. Let's go to The Blue Note."

"No!" Kate screamed. "The kids are at the Sorensons'."

"Why not go there? Why not give me that?"

"Please, no. I have a really nice dinner waiting. I took off the afternoon."

"A nice dinner! You went there with him? You fucked him in some sleazy Old Town hotel and walked there? Is that it?"

"Not in Old Town. Not sleazy. We just ended up there."

"You *drove* to The Blue Note? You picked it out? Jesus, Kate. How could you?"

"I don't know. I let it happen."

"Drive there now! It's the only thing I'm going to do to hurt you back."

"Can I hug you?"

"No! Drive! We'll see what's left after we stew in your shit. Jesus, Kate, fucking Jesus."

She tries to push all the memories away. How do I help him, she wonders. She will watch the moon, free of clouds, all the way to Eureka. That might help. She has done things like that before to clear her mind.

The lumber mill at 299 and 101 skims over tule fog lying low, shining bright over the pastures. She had sped up without noticing. A strangely gratifying sadness lightens her foot on the gas pedal, as if the beauty of their place softens the edges of a painful story she is watching from outside herself. After Arcata, she seems to coast past white caps on the bay, through the lines of eucalyptus, in fog so low she can see over it to the lights of Eureka. In less than ten minutes, she will be there.

IN THE STREET KAL FISHES for his keys and watches David drift down the sidewalk. A car slows down next to David but doesn't stop. It is Kate's. In the soft glow of the streetlights, Kal can see her acknowledge him with a little nod and a quick wave as he turns right in a hurry. She coasts through the intersection, pulls over, and parks behind his car. She gets out, walks toward him, and stops a few feet in front of him.

"Were you planning to join us?"

"I don't know." She is shaking her head, trying to smile.

"Then why did you come?"

"Maybe to watch from outside."

He pushes his hands into the pockets of his overcoat. "That's all?"

"I thought about coming in and sitting beside you."

"Like a final choice, for David to see?"

"I made that before."

"When?"

"Not at one moment. It has been coming."

"How far along is it?"

She takes a step toward him. "Like I said, I already made it."

"I'm never sure. Most of the time you are vague about us."

"Have I been vague with what I show?" she asks, taking another step. "It shouldn't be all that uncertain."

"Nothing is ever certain, even when it seems to be, like we were at first." He pulls his hands from his pockets, fiddles with his keys, leans against his car.

"I guess we've learned that," she says. "Let's go home and make love."

"We need to do other things. More important things."

"Lots," she answers, "but let's do it anyway."

"Stay with the easy stuff?"

"For now. For tonight."

He nods. "See you there." He watches her walk to her car.

STAYING IN SIGHT OF EACH OTHER, they hurry north on 101, toward home. The sky is empty of clouds, the high moon is nearly full, and only small patches of fog hang thin and wispy over road and bay and pasture. The mountains stand dark over the crystal lowlands, darker than the sky. They both know they will raise the blinds for this light. No fire in the living room or candle beside the bed, only the moonlight. She knows she will be all over him from the start, knows he will feast on every part of her, entering her every way he can think of. She will welcome him wherever he goes. He will wonder will she open herself to him with more than her body, she whether they will pay enough attention to each other in the long run, and how long will they try? He will think that if he can get deep enough inside her, some silent, womb-like state might fill him and end his growing desire to reclaim her body as if it were his home that another had seized or that she had given away. She will know that is what he is trying to do. She will shut her inner eye to David. That, she knows that she can do.

On the way home, Kate in the lead, they wonder whether they may be thinking the same thoughts. That without real work, time will work against them, not for them. That tonight they will be hoping, crazily, that wild sex will begin the bridge to some unshaped solid ground on the other side. Something they might call, after the empty years, love. One thing is certain. They won't think about whether it will or won't, or what forgiving and forgetting will require. Not tonight. Tomorrow perhaps, but not tonight.

UNCLE ENO'S BAD DAY

I EASED MY CAR TO A STOP by a rusty gas pump and took a big breath. I could relax now and take a moment to catalog my morning of mistakes: first, passing up rows of neon signs that shouted multiple gas opportunities to anyone paying the slightest attention; then, in near panic over the prospect of missing a department meeting, skipping a half dozen exit ramps that promised more hopeful roads than the one I took; last, after a long half-hour with the fuel light shouting, taking an exit to an unlined two-lane that disappeared into the hardwood forests of North Carolina's Piedmont, offering no more promise than a few scattered fields of tobacco. An irresistible force had prevented me from U-turning to the freeway before it was out of sight. I did not want this choice to be a mistake.

Try something new, I had thought. Bank on faith. A station would appear. With an egg-shell touch on the gas pedal, I babied the car through three long miles in a tunnel of trees, certain, in spite of my new-found faith, that the corridor would outlast the tank. Now, at a no-name station under a stifling mid-day sun that had turned the sky pasty white, I felt saved. My kind of saved. More than an hour remained to reach Durham in time for my three o'clock meeting, a comfortable margin for a car that would no longer be sucking fumes. I stopped cursing myself for not filling up at the gas arcade, thanked whatever for its possible blessing, opened the window, and vowed to never let this happen again.

A massive spreading oak at the edge of the station's asphalt shaded my car. Across the steaming blacktop, not thirty feet away, a low-built one-story cross between a home and a gas station crouched at the wrong edge of the oak's canopy. Its tarpaper roof pulsed waves of heat. To the left of a well-holed screen door, a bald-headed old man sat statue-still in an out-of-place plastic deck chair. Rivers of creases lined his forehead, and a thin white beard scragged from his chin and cheeks. With bony fingers laced around the wooden end of an inverted golf club, he seemed stuck in a forward lean that could outlast the narrow, crumbling veranda. His eyes were as motionless as the rest of him.

A heavyset young man appeared at the door and crossed the veranda at a pace to fit the oven heat. With surprising care, his arms held out from his sides for balance, he came down the only step and began a labored walk toward my car. Dragging his right foot along the asphalt before urging it off the ground, he could not match the length of his stride from that side with the other. His hands hung away from his hips as if he were waiting for something significant to happen, like an athlete anxious for the play to begin. When he reached the side of my car, he supported himself by stiffening one arm against the frame of the back side window, politely out of my line of sight. I had to twist around to see him. From below, his round unblemished face seemed as innocent as a shy teenager's. In spite of its puffiness, it was a handsome face.

"Wha' for ya?" he asked in a toneless voice, his words spoken to the roof of the car.

"A full tank," I said. "It should take more than fourteen. You can top it off. I want to see how much."

"Yessir," he said without looking down, his voice only a whisper.

"Coming down this road was an act of desperation. Can't tell you how relieved I am to find you way out here in this forest."

Even in the deep shade, with the air conditioner off the heat came on like a switch had been flipped. As I got out the young man rotated toward the pump as if he were tethered to a post by a short brace.

"This heat's like being in the bottom of a fish tank," I said. "I bet it's ninety-five in the shade, and the humidity's got to be near a hundred. Might as well be India."

"Is...only...reglar...we got." His words lacked the musical rise and fall I had learned to love about Southern speech. "Low...for engine like this'n."

"Gotta take what you have," I said. "Thought I was running out for sure. The needle was an eighth of an inch below empty, and the fuel light's been on for half an hour. I bet I missed a dozen stations, and then there was nothing. Carolina's funny that way. Lots of everything that's anywhere else and in a blink it looks like you'll never see a sign of life again."

He pulled the nozzle back, drawing a slow circle wide around him. The back of his tee shirt said "Schlitz, The Beer That Made Milwaukee Famous." A sweating brown bottle of cold beer, its icy contents about to pour onto County Stadium's bright green turf, got me wishing for relief.

"Where'd you get that shirt? Schlitz hasn't been around since the Braves moved to Atlanta. I'm sure it never got all the way down here."

He pointed the nozzle toward the closed door to the gas tank. "I...need ya...t'open that."

I reached into the window and yanked the latch beside the bottom of the door. "Sorry. I'm still thinking about getting stuck out here in all these trees. So many trees."

He looked out over the top of the pump.

"I went to Milwaukee once," I said. "Had a Schlitz in that ballpark."

"Wherezat?"

"Wisconsin."

"Wherezat?"

"Oh, up North."

He turned toward me. "Y'all...ferget...to fill up there?" A big grin filled his face.

"No more than anywhere else, I hope," I answered with a chuckle. "It's just me. I forget things when I'm in a hurry. Almost paid for it, but you're here, so I got off lucky."

"Always...been here."

He looked over his shoulder. A second gas pump stood in a sideways tilt at the back end of the asphalt. It was more rust than paint and had no hose. Most of the glass was gone, and a tight pattern of bullet holes filled its chest.

"Once Uncle Eno...dint take nuff time, an' he paid a lot for it." He did a quarter turn back and gazed again over the top of the car, at the stiff old man called Eno. "There he set...twenty year."

"Really?" I asked.

He nodded in long, thoughtful ups and downs, full of effort.

"Can I get to Durham by three o'clock?" I asked. "I have a meeting I can't be late for."

"Take...40."

"That's what I figured. So, maybe an hour?"

With effort the young man twisted away from me, keeping his hand on the nozzle grip, one of those ancient ones lacking a trigger latch. Bending toward the pump, he propped his free arm against it and squinted, seeming to measure the distance to Durham. He turned back scratching an armpit. His shirt there was more hole than material.

"Might could," he said, turning back toward the pump and watching the tenths of gallons creep upward as if studying them mattered. After nearly half a minute, his gaze turned down toward the nozzle, and he concentrated on it in the same way. I knew then for sure that he could only do one thing at a time.

"Uncle Eno's backhoe," he said, pointing toward the back of the asphalt. "It took a month a minutes for fillin'...over there at the diesel." His arm, thick and round and brown as link sausage, swung rigid as a mechanical gate toward the abandoned pump. "Momma say...he never hurry...always pay attention...till the bad day. After that...went back to not hurryin'...right quick, they say. Now he still as a cat that's full. Go in for breakfast...supper...nightfall. That's all. Nothin' but."

I stared at the side of his face. He was working his lips. I waited.

"Only thirteen nine," he said when the numbers stopped. The cadence of his speech had increased as he got into a story he must have known too well. "After he gas up, Uncle Eno always went reverse first, to clear the store on turnin'. Backhoe too big. Seat can turn clear round if you want it to, but he dint. Nary look back. Dint go slow like suppose, and poorly for not lookin'. He still payin'. Settin' an' leanin', eyes on the spot where he done it. Cain't run anyone down sittin' agin a wall. Twenty year, my momma say. I don't rember. Was a tyke."

The young man returned the nozzle to its slot in the pump. He turned his back to me, faced the spot he was talking about, and stayed that way as if he were watching whatever had happened twenty years before. I decided that it was mostly the heat that made him move and speak like a lugging car, or I wished it, and I tried not to worry about my meeting. Turning to look at the old man, I noticed that he, too, was staring toward the dead pump, or off to the right of it. I couldn't tell for sure. Something was out there for him.

I drew a twenty from my wallet and extended it toward the young man.

He began rubbing his index fingers with his thumbs.

"Willa Jane behind. Pullin' at her skirt. Stuck in the bike. Chain, probly. Only five. Singin', Momma say. Nursey rhyme. Uncle dint see. Might should, but should ain't seein'. Big wheel squashed Willa Jane top to bottom. His only granchile. Momma say she still looked sweet, but that's what she wants ta hold."

The young man turned and took the twenty. It seemed like he was reading its numbers. "Thanks, there," he said.

"Quite a story," I said. "Do you tell it to everyone?"

The young man stuffed the twenty in a pocket of his baggy trousers. Through pursed lips that struggled to hide a wiser smile than the innocent grin that had brightened his face before, he stared at me, eye to eye, as if he understood something that he thought still escaped me.

"Not...everyone," he said. Then he turned and hobbled off. "Have...a good day now."

I looked toward the sagging veranda for a last glimpse at Uncle Eno holding himself up on his inverted golf club, and at the young man walking away with an effort that matched his speech. I followed the old man's frozen gaze to the spot that had demanded his attention for twenty years and tried to imagine him hurrying, for the first time, at backing up to make the turn in the too-small space. That's all I tried to see.

In the car the digital clock on my dashboard flashed 2:02, fifty-eight minutes to get to the north side of Durham. Cranking up the engine and lingering there, I saw in the two-lane's mirage of heat the faceless gas stations I had passed, any one of which would have gotten me to my meeting with time to spare, and the tunnel of trees on the turn I had chosen in desperation, never expecting it to save me. Now it looked like it might have.

The frozen old man loomed over the road. Then the young one replaced him. I decided to believe that the younger had been staying at that gas station with the elder for quite some time, that he had the patience it would take to remain there a long time more, and that he would tell the story of Uncle Eno's bad day to more wrong-turn people like me.

Without looking back, I crept out from under the shade of the oak and turned onto the two-lane toward the uncompromising sun. The clock gave me only fifty-five.

ACKNOWLEDGEMENTS

Many thanks are in order. First, to my good friends and marvelous responders in the Mad River Writers' Cooperative: Leslie Dutra, Steve Henry, Mashaw McGinnis, Kathy Marshall, Mack Owen, Trish Raleigh, and Helen Sise. Their insightful criticism, directly but gently delivered (and often humorously), challenged me and helped me take my stories to much better places. Their good cheer and delightful wordplay enrich many dinners out whenever a month has a third Tuesday. That a writing group can become bring such warmth and affection to the solitariness of composing stories is truly a gift.

To Carolyn Mueller, my line-by-line editor who became a terrific responder in her own right, bringing truth to the message of a poet I admire. It was Vinnie Peloso who I heard say, "You don't have to be a writer to be a good responder." Carolyn proves him right. She sees sentences like a hawk, knows the conventions of language backwards and forwards and inside out, and is thorough beyond what I thought possible.

To Carolan Raleigh-Halsing, daughter of the afore-mentioned Trish Raleigh. She blessed me with three beautiful paintings for the front and back covers of this collection and the one soon coming. Those paintings now adorn a wall in my living room. More important, in a single reading of the cover stories, Carolan captured the vision I had in mind for *Filling Up In Cumby* and, for *Last Night At The Vista Café*, found something even better than what I saw.

To Dan Eberhard and Dave Harvey, two very close writing buddies who live too far away for me to properly enjoy. When we can, we talk for hours about each other's writing - the ways we put stories on the pages and the places we find them. Every day I wish these two were closer.

To the creators of the Lost Coast Writers' Retreat: Michael Bickford, Linda Hirsch, Will Hirsch, Cindy Kuttner, Dan Levinson, Vinnie Peloso, Bob Sizoo, and the late Guy Kuttner. For nearly a decade we have worked together to create, recreate, organize, and manage a summer week of heartfelt writing, responding, dining, and playing along the Mattole River on the Northcoast of California. (We intend to retreat there on our walkers.) Following the advice of the afore-mentioned Guy Kuttner, we transformed an allegedly business concern, with all its attendant distractions, to a simple gathering of writing friends and their writing friends. We miss Guy every time, and in all the space in between.

For a third time, to three who give their ears and thoughts to my stories more often than a writer should expect of friends: Lynnette Chen and Geri Anne Johnson, my fellow Gemini ex-lawyers, and Tobin Rangdrol, my son.

Last but not least, to Bonny Jean Johnson, daughter of Geri named above, for reminding me how meaningful a piece of fiction can be when it goes straight to the heart.

ABOUT THE AUTHOR

Jim Steinberg lives close to his children, grandchildren, and friends in beautiful Humboldt County, on the Northcoast of California, Behind The Redwood Curtain. He is the author of one novel, *Boundaries*, is soon to complete his second collection of stories, *Last Night At The Vista Cafe*, and has begun work on *The Third Floor*, his second novel. His stories have appeared in *Clapboard House, The Greensboro Review, tnr (The New Renaissance), Sensations Magazine, Cities and Roads, The Lone Wolf Review, The Bishop's House Review, Voices From Home - A North Carolina Prose Anthology*, and *Best Of Clapboard House*.

Jim is a Fellow of the Redwood Writing Project of Humboldt State University and a founding member of the Lost Coast Writers' Retreat, a six-day gathering along the Mattole River on the remote Northcoast of California. He has taught English and Social Studies in public schools, practiced law, and worked with legal studies and law enforcement training programs in community colleges in the West and the South. For the last twelve years he has been a mediator specializing in helping couples separate, divorce, and settle child custody concerns and property division in a peaceful, collaborative manner. He does this in the reassuring setting of his home and in tribal courts in Northern California. Mediation is his loved vocation, but his avocation, writing fiction, has first place in his heart, save for the family and friends who fill his life.

47381267R00100

Made in the USA
Charleston, SC
07 October 2015

IN FILLING UP IN CUMBY, JIM STEINBERG follows his characters' challenges with a gentle touch. In the title story, when a father's ex-wife appears at an inappropriate time, he struggles to protect their son from his difficulty keeping a healthy distance from the woman who still fascinates him. In "That Girl," a mother cooking dinner for her live-in boyfriend must persuade him to soften his harsh approach to her pregnant fifteen-year-old daughter. In "Uncle Eno's Bad Day," a gas station attenadant with more wits than meets the eye delivers an important lesson about what matters and what does not to a man worried about being late for a meeting.

Steinberg describes our most common struggles and celebrates even the smallest triumphs. He aims to see the struggles with compassion and grace and the triumphs with scrupulous realism.

Jim's stories have appeared in Clapboard House, The Greensboro Review, The New Renaissance, Sensations Magazine, Cities and Roads, The Lone Wolf Review, The Bishop's House Review, Voices From Home - A North Carolina Prose Anthology, and Best Of Clapboard House. He is the author of Boundaries, a novel, and Last Night at the Vista Café, a second collection of stories. He is working on a second novel, Reunion.

Jim lives close to his children, grandchildren (see pictur... and friends in beautiful ... boldt County on the No... coast of California, behi... Redwood Curtain.

ISBN 9781494925444

90000

From Acorns To Angels

The Diary Of A Tree

SAMUEL H. WALLACE